THE RELUCTANT ASSASSIN

THE RELUCTANT ASSASSIN

A Western Story

PRESTON DARBY

Five Star • Waterville, Maine

First Edition
First Printing: December 2005

Published in 2005 in conjunction with Golden West Literary Agency.

Set in 11 pt. Plantin by Minnie B. Raven.

Printed in the United States on permanent paper.

Library of Congress Cataloging-in-Publication Data

Darby, Preston.
    The reluctant assassin : a western story / by Preston Darby.—1st ed.
        p. cm.
    ISBN 1-59414-151-7 (hc : alk. paper)
    1. Booth, John Wilkes, 1838–1865—Fiction. 2. Fugitives from justice—Fiction.   3. Diaries—Authorship—Fiction.   4. Assassins—Fiction. 5. Mummies—Fiction.   6. Texas—Fiction.   I. Title.
PS3604.A724R45 2005
    813'.6—dc22   2005023581

To Pam, with love

And the wild regrets, and the bloody sweats
None know so well as I.
For he who lives more lives than one
More deaths than one must die.

"The Ballad of Reading Gaol"
Oscar Wilde

PROLOGUE

"What I want to know is . . . is it human?"

In fifty years of medical practice I had encountered many peculiar experiences, but the most bizarre event occurred soon after I retired. It involved a man long dead, a man known to history as John Wilkes Booth.

Ken Casper, long-time friend, neighbor, and noted author, had recently acquired some long-abandoned ranch property along the sluggish Concho River near San Angelo and was busy renovating a dilapidated rock storage building.

Ken soon recognized a disparity in the measurements of two walls enclosing an interior room and suspected a concealed space between the partitions. When he had initially confided his suspicions to me, we had jokingly speculated over the possibility of hidden treasure. From the tone of Ken's voice when he phoned me to come out right away, however, I knew whatever he'd found wasn't treasure and it had rattled him.

"I don't know what it is," he answered my first question, his voice half an octave higher than usual. "Come see for yourself."

Ken had been correct in his measurements. A double wall had been constructed between the rooms. Fragments of white limestone and mortar were piled below a manhole-size opening Ken had pick-axed through one wall. Without a word of explanation he handed me a flashlight and stepped back.

I hesitated. "What about snakes?"

Ken clucked his tongue. "With all the racket I've been making around here the last few days, any snakes have crawled to Mexico by now. Look in there off to the right."

I flicked on the light and stuck my arm in the hole, then cautiously inserted my head and peered in the direction of the beam. Motes of dust obscured the flashlight's rays, and at first I saw only the outline of an old wooden chair and what looked like a deteriorating black suit draped over it. I raised the beam slightly and jerked back so quickly I struck my head on one of the protruding bricks. There was something in the suit—something with shrunken hands protruding from the coat sleeves. Curiosity overcame my apprehension and I squeezed through the opening, then played my light up and down the apparition.

"My God, Ken, it's a mummy."

Ken snorted. "I figured that. What I want to know is . . . is it human?"

"Hold on, let me get a better look."

I moved closer to the mummy. The withered hands certainly appeared human, four fingers—or what was left of them—and an opposing thumb. I attempted to move one of the hands from its resting place on the figure's pants leg. With a whispery sound the entire arm separated from the shoulder, decayed cloth fell away, and I dropped the creature's bony appendage as swiftly as if I had grabbed a rattler.

I forced myself to be calm, then squatted and focused my light where I expected the mummy's face should be. The neck was flexed, but enough flesh adhered to the skull for me to know the discovery was human. As I backed out of the opening, I picked up the loose arm and called out to Ken.

"Congratulations. You've found a real human mummy. Here, let me give you a hand." I extended the withered remnant out to him.

Ken recoiled, his eyes wide. "Oh, great. You've really screwed up now. I've written enough detective novels to know better than to disturb a crime scene."

I reached inside the opening and laid the arm back in the mummy's lap.

Ken nodded. "Oh, that'll help."

"We don't know this is a crime scene," I said. "Whoever he is, he's been in there for decades. Maybe he's a relative of somebody who owned this place. He was dressed, placed carefully in the chair, and walled in. So somebody went to a lot of trouble to hide him, right?"

"No doubt about that." Ken shook his head slowly and walked over to sit on the window sill. "But what am I supposed to do? Wall him up again? That's like Poe's 'Cask of Amontillado'."

"Aw, Ken, that's a murder story. I'd bet this guy was dead long before he was put in there. Anyway, we have to call the justice of the peace. First, he has to pronounce him dead"—I smiled wryly—"though that shouldn't tax the JP's neurons too much, and then he'll probably order a forensic autopsy. The pathologist will try to identify the body, determine cause of death, find any evidence of foul play, get tissue samples for DNA testing. . . ." I trailed off, embarrassed at my oration, and shrugged. "What am I doing telling you about all this? You know the procedure better than I do and make a dern' good living writing about it."

"Just listening to see if you know your stuff." Ken grinned and rose from his perch at the window. "Now let's go call the JP and see if he knows his."

11

After a cursory examination and considerable deliberation, our justice of the peace concluded that Ken's mummy was indeed dead and could be removed to Foster's Funeral Home. Attempts to encompass the mummy in a standard receptacle resulted in frustration for the attendants and further minor trauma to the body. Therefore, he was seated on a chair in the cooler to await the arrival of a forensic pathologist from San Antonio, the esteemed Dr. Nasir Taboor.

Three weeks passed. Only a small paragraph mentioning the mummy's discovery made our San Angelo *Standard Times*. Somehow the newspaper's brief account was relegated to the sports section.

Then I received a phone call from an uncharacteristically excited Ken Casper.

"Pres. I'm picking you up in five minutes. The pathologist just called. I could hardly understand the man's accent, but he said he had found something 'veeery interrrresting' in the mummy. See you."

He hung up before I could speak.

Except for the unpretentious lighted sign on the front lawn, Foster's Funeral Home could have easily been mistaken for any upscale colonial residence. Lush manicured lawns and meticulously trimmed shrubbery surrounding the edifice provided a sharp contrast to the usual potted cacti and concrete landscaping of downtown San Angelo.

Dr. Taboor had been given a small office to use while dictating his findings, and responded to our knock with a heavily accented: "Enter. Enter, please."

After brief introductions, the gnome-like little doctor with tiny manicured hands bade us to—"Sit, sit."—and almost disappeared behind the desk when he returned to his seat.

"Now you, Mister Casper, are the owner of this mummy, is that true?"

"I guess so," Ken answered guardedly. "I found it, but I've not talked to a lawyer about the legalities yet."

"I suggest you do so, sir, because of the very interesting findings in this case, you see." Taboor leaned back in his chair, obviously enjoying the suspense he was creating. "Let me summarize."

He placed a pair of ridiculously large horn-rimmed glasses on his prominent nose making him appear more hobbit-like than ever. After shuffling through a sheaf of papers on his desk for an exasperatingly long time, he began to read. "The mummy is an adult male without evidence of significant external trauma sufficient to cause his demise. There is an old well-healed fracture of the left fibula and a surgical scar on the posterior neck. His left arm has been recently separated from the shoulder. An old scar is present in the right eyebrow region and some deformity of the right thumb is present, probably secondary to a previous injury. The body is remarkably well preserved in a state of mummification."

Taboor looked up from his papers and removed his glasses. "That's probably because of the arid west Texas climate, as well as being hermetically sealed, so to speak, away from insects, animals, and such." He perched the glasses back on his nose, pursed his lips in a sly smile, and returned to his notes.

"Now for the good part. A lengthy Y-shaped surgical scar extends caudally from the infra-clavicular areas to the xiphoid process and thence to the symphysis pubis. This incision was made post-mortem and roughly sutured." Taboor squinted over his glasses at us and smiled wickedly. "All internal organs have been removed."

Ken leaned over and whispered: "What did he just say?"

"Somebody gutted him like a hog." Ken's shocked expression indicated that my reply should be less graphic and more clinical, so I added: "I would suspect someone removed his insides to prepare the body for mummification."

Taboor shifted impatiently in his chair. "If you please, gentlemen, I have not finished." He paused until our attention was completely focused on him, and cleared his throat. "From the abdominal cavity, I removed this." He reached into a drawer to produce an obviously heavy thick rectangular-shaped object wrapped in oiled leather, and placed it dramatically on the desk.

"My God," Ken exclaimed. "It's a book."

The three of us stood and stared at the package for a moment.

"I did not open the wrapping," said Dr. Taboor, "for presumably you are the rightful owner and should have that privilege."

Ken needed no further encouragement, and slowly removed the fragile covering. "It looks like some sort of journal," he murmured, "and there's something written on the front." He moved the desk lamp closer and bent over the book. "A True Account," he read, "by JWB. What do you make of that, Pres?"

"I've always heard every man has a book in him."

Ken and Dr. Taboor groaned.

"But seriously, folks," I offered lamely. "This does look like someone's journal or diary. Ken, I'd suggest you make sure you're the legal owner before opening it."

"I certainly agree, sir," Dr. Taboor chimed in. "This is why I left it sealed, you see. I have obtained X-rays, dental films, and tissue samples for DNA testing which may help us to identify the mummy, but examination of this book could be crucial."

"OK, OK." Ken raised his hands in mock protest. "I knew I'd need a lawyer sooner or later. Now I'll have to find out what to do with this book and the mummy."

We thanked Dr. Taboor, and I sat in the foyer idly turning the pages of an old *National Geographic* while Ken phoned his lawyer from an adjoining office. Like an unbidden refrain—*JWB—mummy, mummy—JWB*—echoed in my brain. What was the connection?

"We're all set, Pres," Ken said as he entered, his face glowing. "Tom Davis says if I found the items on property legally owned by me, and there are no heirs to make a claim, the items are mine. I bought the land in a bank auction and the title is clear, so there are no other claimants. Tom's going to send me a document with all the whereases and wherefores just in case, but says it's OK to examine the journal and . . . dispose of the mummy."

"Mummy . . . JWB," I murmured.

"What?"

"I've got it."

"Got what?"

"The connection. JWB . . . John Wilkes Booth, it's his journal." I stood up, trembling. "The mummy. . . ."

"Oh, come on, Pres, be serious," Ken interrupted. "Booth was killed in a barn somewhere in Virginia a couple of weeks after he shot Lincoln. How could a dead man write a diary?"

"Wait, listen. This time I'm not joking. When I was in high school, I wrote a term paper on Booth. Lots of people claim he escaped and ended up living in Texas."

"Surely, you jest," Ken said wryly.

"No, really. And I remember my grandmother telling me

when she was a young girl, she saw a mummy at a county fair that was supposedly John Wilkes Booth." I almost laughed at Ken's incredulous expression. "Wait, there's more. Booth's diary was supposedly found on his body after he was shot. So what's this?" I pointed at the volume.

"Hold on, hold on, old buddy. This time I'm calling your bluff. I'll get my camera set up at home to photocopy this journal as we read it before it falls apart, and we'll go through the entire document, page by page."

Ken shook his head at me and grinned. "Every man has a book in him. You ought to be ashamed."

True to his word, Ken had rigged his digital camera over a small table in his study and clamped a flood lamp on the tripod. The journal had been removed from its leather case and lay unopened under the apparatus. Ken reached to un-clasp the cover, then paused dramatically. "I have a bad feeling we're opening a real can of worms here, whatever we find."

I nodded in agreement, feeling a little uneasy myself. "But my curiosity is killing me."

Ken opened the book and adjusted his spotlight. Al-though the journal's pages were fragile and yellowed with age, the spidery handwriting was distinct and legible. Ken's prediction was confirmed in the first sentence.

BOOK ONE

Fear that man who fears not God.

Abd-el-kader

CHAPTER ONE

I never intended to kill Abraham Lincoln.

I detested the old gorilla and his fawning sycophants, but was wise enough to know that he was much more valuable to our Cause as a pawn rather than a martyr.

So much drivel has been written concerning the events of April 14, 1865, and the weeks following, that I feel compelled to furnish this accurate narrative. After all, who should know the true story better than I? And at my present stage in life, I have no reason to lie.

Early in 1864, it was manifest to me that the South's chances of effecting further stunning military successes and a negotiated peace were fading. Despite our best clandestine efforts the New York Draft Riots had not resulted in widespread demands by the Northern populace that Lincoln end the war. Even our fire-bombing of several hotels in New York City had not terrified the residents of that accursed city as we had hoped, and unfortunately only resulted in the capture and hanging of Robert Kennedy, one of our most valuable operatives.

I, therefore, concluded that our only salvation was a dramatic event which would demonstrate the hidden weaknesses of the Yankee government and the steadfast resolve of my beloved Confederacy.

We would kidnap President Lincoln, race to Richmond, and place him in the custody of authorities there. His release would be contingent on his despicable accomplices ending the war and recognizing the independent states of the Confederacy. To harm or kill Lincoln would be self-defeating and monumentally stupid. If I had truly wanted to murder him, I could have easily accomplished this task during his inauguration on March 4th. I am an excellent marksman and was positioned just above and behind him during his address, affording an elegant opportunity and a clear shot. But I harbored no desire to martyr this man or myself.

I am not at heart an assassin. What I did was done on my part with purely patriotic motives, believing, as I was eventually persuaded at that time, that the death of President Lincoln and the succession of Vice President Johnson, a Southerner from Tennessee, was the only hope for the South.

For more than a fortnight I had argued vehemently against any attempt at assassination, and in fact organized several attempts to kidnap the President. But faulty intelligence information, which I now know was intentional, thwarted every effort. The incompetence and downright stupidity of those whom I was forced to employ played no small part in our failures.

Notwithstanding these disasters, I continued to recommend kidnapping and initially refused to abide any discussion of alternatives in my scenario to eliminate Lincoln. My feelings on this subject did not change even after publication of incriminating documents found on Union Colonel Dahlgren detailing the federal government's plot to murder our President Jefferson Davis.

However, unforeseen matters beyond my control forced me to alter this view.

On the 9th of April, 1865, our beloved General Lee surrendered. Not because he succumbed to the overwhelming forces arrayed against him, but to rescue his valiant troopers from starvation and death. The surrender of General Johnson and the remaining Confederate armies would soon follow. Therefore, kidnapping Lincoln to force a negotiated peace was no longer a viable option. Even if our current plans for his abduction had proved successful, the Confederate government in Richmond had collapsed, and there would be no official means of negotiation.

However, our plans for a kidnapping continued, for we hoped to bargain Lincoln's release, unharmed, for more favorable treatment of the defeated Confederate States. I was unaware of any change in intent until just prior to an afternoon meeting with my colleagues at Washington's Kirkwood Hotel on April 14th to finalize our plans for that evening.

We had learned through our sources that President and Mrs. Lincoln would be attending this evening's performance at Ford's Theatre. During intermission after the second act, a White House messenger would enter the box and tell the President that his presence was needed immediately at the War Department. His guards would have been lured away on a ruse, chloroformed, and replaced by our men.

The President, and Mrs. Lincoln if she refused to stay at the theatre, would be rushed to his carriage and escorted by a troop of horsemen disguised as Union cavalry to the homes of Secretary of State Seward and Vice President Johnson. These notables would be forced to enter the carriage with the threat that the President would be killed immediately if they did not comply.

The entourage would then proceed into Maryland via the Navy Yard Bridge and be loaded onto a ship waiting at Benedict's Landing on Chesapeake Bay. Such an outrageous plot seemed doomed to fail, but my reasoned objections were overruled by that idiot, James William Boyd, who had been designated agent in charge by Confederate sympathizers funding our venture.

Earlier that day I had learned that General and Mrs. Grant would be seated in the same box as the Lincolns, security measures would be even tighter, and the plan could not possibly succeed. I would attend our meeting only to inform the others I wanted no further rôle in this harebrained scheme.

No one had arrived at our selected meeting room in the Kirkwood Hotel, so I repaired to the comfortable bar for a small glass of brandy. One drink is never enough for me, for I staunchly believe the old maxim: "Anything worth doing is worth doing to excess."

As I sipped my third glass, feeling quite mellow, an immaculately attired Union officer armed with sheathed saber and holstered pistol approached my table. Without uttering a word, he handed me a note and waited until I opened the envelope and read.

If you value your own life and the lives of your fellow conspirators, accompany my messenger.

It was unsigned.

Curiosity and the brandy overcame my momentary fear. I downed the remains of my glass and followed the silent officer up several flights of stairs and into the anteroom of a lavish suite. He motioned for me to be seated, then closed the door behind him as he exited into an adjoining bedroom. I had scarcely taken my seat in a plush, overstuffed chair when the officer returned followed by a man I recognized instantly.

Until I am confident this manuscript can be properly secured following its completion, I shall refer to this gentleman as Z. Suffice it to say that I had met this high governmental official over a year ago in Nashville after my performance in a play and had recognized him at several events in Washington. Coarse in manner and appearance, rough in speech, he was by birth a Southerner, but by no means a gentleman. I had never seen him completely sober, and he exhaled cheap liquor with his greeting.

"By God, Booth, we've got you and your bunch in the cross-hairs now, and I mean to pull the trigger. You're the single person in your gang with enough sense to be of any use to me . . . the rest can hang for all I care. One of your cohorts"—an evil smile creased his face—"with a little encouragement and to save his own hide has confessed to your dastardly plot to kidnap the President. I can probably save this man from the noose, but I would offer you a better bargain." The boorish man's pig-like eyes narrowed to slits. "I know you as an accomplished actor, Booth, but let me warn you, don't try to bluff me."

"What do you want me to do?"

Even the most skilled thespian could not have concealed his shock at this vermin's answer.

"Tonight, I want you to kill Lincoln."

Evil exuded from this man like a vapor as he informed me that I would perpetrate this monstrous act or be killed on the spot by his armed guard, Colonel Browning. Investigators would be told that Browning was defending Z from my insane attack.

Recovering my speech if not my equanimity, I protested that an attack on Lincoln at Ford's Theatre would surely fail and would be suicidal. Not only Lincoln's bodyguards, but a military contingent protecting General and Mrs. Grant would surround the Presidential box. Even if the attempt should prove successful, there could be no escape through the narrow corridors and passageways of the theatre.

If, by some miracle, I could escape the theatre, all bridges from Washington were constantly guarded by soldiers who allowed no one to exit the city without a secret password. As a matter of fact, my young companion, David Herold, and I had recently been detained for hours at the Navy Yard Bridge before being allowed entry into the city.

Z smirked, and signaled to Browning. The menacing, silent man immediately poured a tumbler full of bourbon for him from an ample supply on the ornate sideboard. He downed half the glass without wincing, then looked me up and down like a predator readying his kill.

"I dearly love a good old Tennessee fox hunt," he drawled, "but it's boring if the fox has no hope of escape." His ghoulish smile returned. "So let's say I've changed the odds a little."

I then learned that General and Mrs. Grant would not accompany the Lincolns, having received an urgent message that their daughter was ill and required their presence. No guards would be outside the President's box except "my man, Parker" who would be called away at an appropriate time. A password, to be furnished after the deed was done, would satisfy guards stationed at the bridge. There would be other attacks on "the Lincoln bunch" in Washington as a diversionary measure. Once out of the city I would be on my own—"With all the hounds of hell nipping at your heels."

Surely the brandy had confused my reason more than I realized. I felt sure much of what he had told me was false, and he could not allow me to escape once I had killed the President. But I could die knowing I was a martyr to my cause, famous beyond belief. Far better, I decided, than dying here alone, impaled on Browning's saber. This faulty decision would haunt me to my grave.

I rose and swallowed to control my voice. "I have little choice, sir, but to do as you wish. I would ask that you spare my friends, guilty only of. . . ."

"You fool!" Z roared and leaped to his feet, shoving his face close to mine. His breath was foul. "Save your heroics for the stage. I will see you all hang. You, Booth, are being given a chance only because I have need of your detailed knowledge of Ford's Theatre. Accept . . . or face death now."

I dropped to my seat and nodded slowly. The die was cast.

CHAPTER TWO

I sat mute with disgust and horror while this truly evil man detailed his nefarious scheme and the rôle I was doomed to play. Instead of kidnapping, this was murder most foul on an appalling scale. Not only was President Lincoln a target, but also Secretary of State William Seward, and Vice President Andrew Johnson.

"Your man should have no trouble with Seward after he gains access to his room. He is bedridden with recent shoulder and neck injuries. But with Johnson, that is a different story." Z leaned forward, and smiled wickedly. "He is much tougher than most people think. I want you to let me or Colonel Browning know, after your meeting, which of the assassins you select for him. Leave a note with the desk clerk."

I was furnished detailed instructions concerning my escape route from Ford's Theatre to the Navy Yard Bridge, and the password for the guards stationed there. Next, Colonel Browning issued me a Derringer pistol and one .44-caliber lead ball. From my exceptional knowledge of handguns, I knew this weapon to be notoriously inaccurate beyond the range of a few inches. I would have to be practically touching President Lincoln in order to be certain of delivering a lethal wound.

Z dismissed me with a wave of his hand. As I departed, the infernal rascal's final words echoed prophetically in my ears.

"I'll see you in hell, Booth."

The unsavory encounter with these diabolic schemers left me fuming and dangerously close to sober. My anger was soothed to some degree, and the latter affliction remedied by two substantial brandies at the Kirkwood bar. I then strode rapidly to the Herndon House for my meeting with Lewis Paine. This oaf with the strength and brain of an ox only blinked and nodded stupidly when I told him of the change in plans. The proposed kidnapping was cancelled, and he was assigned the task of exterminating Seward at his home. David Herold, the youngest member of our band who idolized me, would accompany Paine to Seward's house, control the horses, while Paine eliminated Seward, and facilitate their escape.

After laboriously repeating several times my instructions to Paine in hopes of achieving some degree of penetration into the blockhead's brain, I returned to the Kirkwood Hotel for my scheduled meeting with George Atzerodt. This immigrant carriage-repairman had been introduced to me at Mary Surratt's boarding house and was persuaded to join our group by promises of cash and liquor. From my acquaintance with him thus far, he was seldom sober and a sniveling coward to boot. His only use to me was his encyclopedic knowledge of the safest escape route through Maryland and the rivers beyond. Now I was compelled at this late juncture to rely on him to assassinate Vice President Johnson, knowing his chances for success were meager to none.

Leaving Atzerodt brooding over his whiskey, I left a note, as instructed, with the desk clerk for Colonel Browning, naming Atzerodt as the potential assassin of Johnson. Now I was on my own, as I preferred it, rather than being further burdened with the incompetence and stupidity of this pathetic band of plotters.

At precisely 4:00 p.m., I rented the fleet mare from Pumphrey's stable I had reserved earlier, and rode unhurriedly to Deery's tavern above Grover's Theatre. There I imbibed a few more draughts of liquid bravado. As I sat silently planning the events of what might well be my last night on this earth, I realized few mere mortals could understand my motivation for the attack on Lincoln. Certainly any newspaper's speculation on my mental processes would be hopelessly distorted. Therefore, I composed a letter outlining my original intent to kidnap the President, and my reasons for abandoning this plan. No mention was made of the encounter with Z, for obvious reasons.

I signed the letter with a flourish, then, with all humility, decided I would share the glory with my compatriots. Beneath my signature I scrawled the names George Atzerodt, Lewis Paine, and David Herold, thus ensuring them a place in history. The last glass of brandy was downed as easily as the several preceding it and I left to post my letter.

As I walked my mare down 14th Street, my mind was preoccupied with details of the coming evening. These thoughts were interrupted by a greeting from a fellow actor, John Matthews. John was playing a rôle in this evening's performance of *Our American Cousin* at Ford's Theatre and requested my expert advice on his interpretation of the rôle. Much to his surprise and profound admiration, I knew almost every line in the play and provided him with several astute recommendations that would certainly enhance his performance. To return my favor, he readily agreed to deliver my letter to the *National Intelligencer* the next day. During our conversation I learned that the loudest laughter in the theatre occurred after a line by the leading man, Harry Hawk, at about 10:15 p.m. I would time my attack on Lincoln to coincide with this noise from the audience.

Bidding Matthews a pleasant evening and best wishes for a successful run of the play, I mounted my steed and met Atzerodt on a side street. The incompetent foreigner was already staggering from alcohol and reluctant to talk with me. I dismounted, braced the fool against a building, and emphasized repeatedly that he should time his attack on Johnson at precisely 10:15, and advise Paine and Herold to arrive at Seward's home at that time. The idiot's reluctance and cowardice left me with an uneasy presentiment that he would botch both tasks.

But it was now nearly 6:00 p.m., and I had much to do in my own preparations. To hell with my incompetent accomplices! At least, I would not fail.

As a consummate thespian, I knew full well that no amount of talent obviated the necessity for rehearsal, and rode to Ford's Theatre to complete preparations for the greatest rôle of my illustrious career.

Although I knew the doors and passageways at Ford's as well as the veins on my hands, I needed to facilitate my entry into the Presidential box and expedite my exit from the building. Some privacy was necessary for my explorations, and there was no problem persuading almost all of the theatre's employees to join me for drinks at Taltavul's Star Saloon. After the first round I excused myself, leaving them happily drinking at my expense, and returned to the theatre.

I paced the route I would use to Lincoln's seat and with a small gimlet drilled a hole in the door to his box so I could ascertain the President's exact location before entering. I prepared a small board to wedge the passageway door closed after I entered the box, thus delaying anyone's entry after the shot, and giving me time to make my leap to the stage below. For one possessing my grace and athletic abilities, such a leap would pose no problem, and I would exit backstage from the theatre to my horse, saddled and waiting in the alley. I retraced every step of my route except the leap several times until I could navigate it blindfolded.

I returned to the saloon and joined the group from Ford's for one final drink, graciously accepted their thanks for my generosity, and returned to the National Hotel for an unusually fine dinner. Unfortunately my excellent meal counteracted the beneficial effects of the brandy, a condition I would remedy as soon as possible—particularly since I would soon face the most unpleasant minutes of this evening: another meeting with the dullards I had been forced to utilize for our assault.

First, I would dress as befitted my reputation and image. I donned an immaculate black suit, calf-length boots and spurs, topping all with a rakish black hat. Inside my coat I secured the loaded Derringer, my diary, a compass, and a large sheathed Bowie knife. I detest knives, but would need some means of defense in close quarters after using the single-shot pistol.

My accomplices and I met in a secluded alley not far from Pumphrey's and remained mounted in order to disperse rapidly if discovered. Once again I detailed our plans in the unlikely hope that my words would somehow penetrate their numb skulls.

Herold would direct Paine to Seward's home, then remain outside with the horses until Paine had dispatched the secretary. Together they would remove themselves to the Navy Yard Bridge.

Atzerodt would knock on Vice President Johnson's door, shoot whoever answered, kill Johnson. and join Herold and Paine.

I would go alone to Ford's Theatre, and then meet them at the bridge. All attacks were to commence at 10:15 p.m. If arrival at the bridge was delayed or unco-ordinated, we would meet at the tavern in Surrattsville, proceed to Port Tobacco on the Maryland shore of the Potomac, cross into Virginia, disperse, and head south.

Following my instructions and the brief discussion that followed, I was convinced that the incompetence of my accomplices would insure that I would never see them again.

The feisty mare trotted briskly through the dimly lit streets of Washington to a dark alley behind Ford's. I dismounted at exactly 9:22 p.m. and left my steed in the care of a young employee of the theatre while I walked next door to Taltavul's. To the surprise of the tavern's bartender I ordered a bottle of whiskey and some water rather than my usual brandy. Before embarking on this night's work, I needed expeditiously to repair damage done to my alcohol level by the recent meal.

This pleasant chore was satisfactorily accomplished in less than a half hour, and I left the tavern for the theatre, entering the lobby shortly after 10:00 p.m. After ascending the stairs to the dress circle, I paused to determine the location of the President's guards in this public area. There was none! I suspected some might be present in mufti, but no one accosted me when I walked casually to the little white door opening into the hallway directly behind Lincoln's box. An empty chair outside the door furnished mute testimony that the President's assigned bodyguard, Parker, had been called away as promised by Z.

I quickly entered the white door, closed it behind me, and wedged the board I had prepared so no one could enter. In the darkness I pressed my eye against the gimlet hole to Lincoln's box and awaited my cue line from the stage.

As Harry Hawk intoned—"Don't know the manners of good society, eh?"—I entered the box a few feet behind Lincoln and moved closer until the Derringer in my extended right hand almost touched his head just below the left ear.

"Wal, I guess I know enough to turn you inside out, you sockdologizing old mantrap."

As a roar of laughter erupted from the audience, I fired.

Reams of newsprint have been filled describing the events that followed. It has been suggested that I uttered some cry or oath. Dramatically *"Sic semper tyrannis"* and "Revenge for the South" are most often attributed to me. In all honesty I must say I do not recall any such expression, but considering the heat of the moment I may be guilty of a lapse of memory.

Vividly imprinted in my brain like a Mathew Brady photograph are the expressions of Mrs. Lincoln, the young officer, and his lady as the President slumped forward. The officer, who I learned later was a Major Rathbone, seized my arm. I dropped the Derringer, drew my knife, and slashed his forearm in self-defense.

He fell back, and I vaulted over the railing. For a moment I hung by my arms before dropping to the stage. As I released my grip, I attempted to turn to my right and face the audience on landing, perhaps thinking to proclaim some words worthy of the occasion. The excitement and the whiskey had so muddled my faculties that my right spur tangled in a flag dangling from the President's box. I landed heavily on my left leg and crumpled to the stage on my outstretched hands.

Strangely I felt no pain and hobbled off the stage past the paralyzed actors and stagehands through the wings to my horse. Vaguely I was aware of cries of—"Stop him, stop him!"—but no one attempted to impede my progress while I brandished my knife.

The mare was skittish and I lay across the saddle as she whirled until I could reach the stirrup with my good leg, mount, and flee through the alleys while a swelling chorus of shouts and curses echoed behind me.

Although I knew my leg was severely injured, I felt little pain and was able to support most of my weight in the right stirrup and by clutching the pommel with my left hand. Rather awkwardly at first, I raced down Pennsylvania Avenue toward the Capitol, then turned into unlighted New Jersey Avenue which bisected a rather disreputable collection of hovels. Reaching Virginia Avenue I turned left, slowed my pace so as not to alert the waiting guards, and arrived at the Navy Yard Bridge a few minutes before 11:00.

The sergeant on duty questioned me briefly and seemed satisfied with my story that I had been delayed in the city past the deadline of 9:00 p.m. and wished to return to my home near Beantown. He never asked for the secret password furnished me by the nefarious Z.

While I eased the mare at a casual pace across the bridge into Maryland, I again congratulated myself that the acting skills I had so carefully honed over many illustrious years had paid off handsomely. But I was not yet safe, far from it. I could urge the mare into a gallop only for a short distance, then she would lag into a trot, or my leg would pain me so I would have to rein her in. The numbing effects of the whiskey had rapidly dissipated, and I desperately needed a drink.

At the crest of a low hill I encountered a lone rider headed toward Washington. In response to my query, he replied that he had not met any horsemen ahead of me, so I knew none of my compatriots had exited the city prior to my departure. I asked him for directions to Marlboro, knowing that, if he were questioned by my pursuers, they would proceed with haste to that village, rather than Surrattsville, my true destination.

Soon after this episode, I heard a rider coming up behind me at a gallop. I hid in a thicket by the road until he went by, then yelled for him to stop. It was David Herold.

He had heard nothing of Atzerodt but was sure Paine had killed Seward. There had been a great commotion in Seward's house, then a servant ran out into the street screaming: "Murder, murder!"

Herold had tied Paine's horse to a tree and fled for his life.

A few minutes after midnight we arrived at Surratt's Tavern. I remained in the saddle while Herold woke the alcoholic John Lloyd, who leased the tavern from Mary Surratt, and asked him to retrieve the package we had left there. My leg was throbbing, and I knew I could not travel much farther without medical attention.

After an eternity the sot returned with our supplies and a quart of whiskey, thank God, allowing me to medicate myself liberally while Herold unwrapped our package. I took the field glasses and told him to leave the carbines. They were too heavy, being government issue, and I could not carry one and use a crutch as well. Herold felt safer keeping his, so I did not argue.

Despite the whiskey, the pain in my left leg had become so severe that it was imperative that I find a doctor immediately rather than sprinting nearly eighteen miles to Port Tobacco on the Potomac as we had planned. The nearest physician was Dr. Mudd in Bryantown, about seventeen miles to the southeast. Dawn was only a few hours away.

Detouring to Mudd's would cost us precious time and delay our arrival at Port Tobacco until after daylight. But even with the beneficial effects of the whiskey, I knew I could not bear the pain in my leg much longer. We would ride for Bryantown.

CHAPTER THREE

We slowed our horses to a walk and rode under pitch-dark starless skies down the sandy road leading to Dr. Mudd's home. I knew this physician to be a man of sterling character and a true Southerner, but if he recognized me and later heard of my involvement in Lincoln's death, he would feel honor bound to report my visit. In addition, the rage and fanaticism of those who pursued me might bring harm to him or anyone who furnished me succor.

Therefore, I donned a false beard from my saddlebag and streaked my face with charcoal, trusting this disguise and my skills as a thespian to transform myself into an injured old man. David Herold was immediately astonished by the metamorphosis. I hoped Mudd could quickly bind or splint my leg so we could leave his house as quickly as possible and resume our flight before dawn.

We would be forced to ride slower on backcountry farm roads to Port Tobacco, but still should arrive before 8:00 a.m., well ahead of the enraged Federals. Atzerodt had been instructed to meet us with a boat, but if this plan went awry, with sufficient financial inducement we should have no problem renting a vessel to cross the river into Virginia and safety.

To complement my deception, I directed David to do most of the talking and coached the lad in his dialogue. He had become a surprisingly apt pupil, seeming to regard our perilous trek as an exciting exploit rather than a matter of life and death.

Shortly after 4:00 a.m. the doctor finally responded to Herold's persistent knocking and cracked the door in his nightshirt, holding a candle. As instructed, David answered Mudd's query by relating that we were traveling to Washington and his friend had taken a tumble from his horse, severely injuring his leg.

David held the candle while Mudd eased me from the saddle and helped me hobble into his parlor.

"You won't get to Washington tonight," he said after a brief examination. "We need to get you upstairs, so I can cut your boot off and see what needs to be done."

By now the pain had become so severe I knew I could go no farther. I came perilously close to swooning while David and Mudd supported me up the stairs to a bedroom. The doctor swiftly incised my boot and slipped it off. A mercifully brief period of poking and probing followed, whereupon the gentle physician diagnosed the fracture and splinted my leg.

Although the pain had lessened to some degree, I could not return to the saddle, and Mudd graciously invited me to rest in his home a few hours. I saw the panic on my young companion's face when this was announced and quickly suggested he tend to our horses.

I dozed fitfully for an hour or so. When David returned, I sent him for a razor so that I might remove my stylishly drooping trademark moustache. On my initial glimpse in the mirror, I recoiled in shock. My locks and moustache were coal-black while the false beard was gray. But Mudd had given no indication that he suspected a disguise. I shaved with great haste and cropped my long hair as best I could with the razor, stuffed the beard in my pocket, and pulled my hat down to my ears.

Prior to his early morning trip to Bryantown, Dr. Mudd

had left instructions with his hired man to fashion wooden crutches for me. These had been fitted and I was hobbling about downstairs when Mudd returned, highly agitated.

In town he had learned of Lincoln's death and encountered several troops of Federal cavalry scouring the roads nearby. Although to this day I do not believe that the man knew me to be Booth, our behavior and appearance were suspicious enough that he ordered us to leave immediately.

I paid the doctor generously for his skill and hospitality, mounted the mare with David's assistance, and we followed a narrow cart road into the eerie gloom of murky Zekiah Swamp. We had been advised to adhere closely to the path to avoid this region's double-barreled lethal threat of quicksand and poisonous snakes. Even patrolling Federal cavalry troops would hesitate to enter the swamp without good reason, and we might be able to regain time lost at Mudd's. The trail would lead us near the shack of Oswald Swann, a Negro man who could guide us safely through this morass to the farm of Samuel Cox, a Confederate sympathizer. From his home we would seek transport across the river into Virginia.

I would pause at this juncture in my narrative to express my profound revulsion at the perfidious judgments meted out to Mrs. Mary Surratt and Dr. Samuel Mudd, innocent victims of a most foul miscarriage of justice. Let me set the record straight, for who better than I knows the true facts?

Mrs. Surratt provided sustenance and lodging for numerous Confederate sympathizers during our War for Southern Independence as was true of many in Maryland at that time. But her service to our Cause ended there. She was never a member of any conspiracy, particularly, as I can readily testify without reservation, the so-called "Lincoln Conspiracy". This innocent woman was torn from her family, imprisoned, and hooded until her trial. Convicted unjustly by perjured testimony, she was hanged *en masse* with three male defendants. No one, no one, especially an innocent Southern lady, is deserving of such scandalous treatment. As the blood of Lincoln besmirches my hands, the blood of Mary Surratt blemishes the hands of those who treated her so despicably.

Dr. Mudd, whose only crime was following the precepts of his Hippocratic oath, remained unjustly imprisoned for years in a vile, fetid pesthole. To this day I am unalterably convinced that Mudd did not recognize me when we arrived at his home begging assistance. I have taken great pride in my monumental success as an actor convincing an audience that I am the character I play. Do you think for a moment that under the circumstances of our encounter I could not have fooled Dr. Mudd? Although we had met in the past, he gave no evidence that he thought of me other than an injured stranger to whom he applied his medical skills with sincere compassion. Would you imprison and punish the Good Samaritan?

For shame, for shame, you liars and hypocrites!

I now resume this narrative with trembling hand, still incensed after the passage of many years at the ghastly treatment of these two compassionate souls whose only crime was following the Golden Rule.

Zekiah Swamp was more forbidding than we had expected. As the evening sunlight waned, limbs intertwined overhead and their dense foliage all but obliterated the fading light. Soon all was dark and we trusted our steeds to keep us on the narrow path that by-passed rotting logs and dank pools of stagnant water.

I would not have seen the man except for the whiteness

and motion of his eyes against the ebony backdrop. He said not a word when I asked directions but pointed down the barely visible trail. Vexed and testy from my throbbing leg, I ordered the Negro, who I assumed to be Swann, to lead us. But he stood, silent and unmoving, until David leveled his carbine and repeated my demand. The man shrugged and climbed aboard a rail-thin mule, tied close by, although I had not seen the beast in this infernal darkness. Swann led us in single file through the swamp for what seemed to be an eternity, but in actuality could only have been several hours. We arrived at the Cox farm shortly before dawn.

Samuel Cox obviously had heard our approach and came out of his house to greet us. While we exchanged introductions and I made our needs known, especially the urgent necessity of leaving this area and crossing the river into Virginia, Swann sat astride his mule, well away from us. Obviously he wanted to avoid any knowledge of our identities or involvement in our plans.

While Cox was most sympathetic to our needs and it was obvious to me that he wished to help, I could readily understand his reservations. Federal patrols were saturating the area and he was already being watched closely, for his past support of the Confederacy was widely known. He showed me one of the handbills which were being distributed throughout this section of Maryland offering the princely sum of $200,000 for my capture. A most unflattering and inaccurate description of me followed, but I derived some solace from the knowledge that no one would recognize me from such a portrayal. The next paragraph contained the warning: **anyone who aids, comforts, feeds, clothes, shelters, or keeps secret the knowledge of the whereabouts of the murderer or of anyone of his fellow conspirators shall be charged as co-conspirators.**

Although not specifically stated on the document, it was obvious that the punishment for this was death. Naturally, regardless of his inner feelings, Samuel Cox could not expose himself or his family to the risk involved in harboring David Herold and me on his premises.

The good man did not banish us as some would have, but referred us to his overseer, Gerald Robey, who lived in a small outbuilding not far from Cox's home. We woke Robey, who paused long enough to resuscitate David and me with food and strong coffee, then led us to a pine thicket a mile or more from his house where we would be concealed until arrangements could be made to ferry us across the river. I wrote a check to him for $300.00 for his services, which he gratefully accepted. Before leaving, Robey demonstrated a whistle that would alert us to the approach of a friend. No whistle, shoot and flee.

I whiled away that sluggish Easter morning writing in my makeshift diary, actually an old notebook I had carried for some time. Regardless of the outcome of future events, I wished to record my thoughts, knowing that newspaper speculations on my mental status and motives for my deeds would be woefully distorted and malicious, containing not a single grain of truth.

I had been writing and dozing for several hours when I was startled by the signal whistle. David crept out of our hide-out and soon returned with a stranger who I learned was Thomas Jones, foster brother of Samuel Cox. Over the next several days, this remarkable and courageous man provided us with food and drink while he watched for an opportunity to smuggle us across the Potomac in his rowboat.

Later I learned that Jones had been in the Confederate Secret Service for three years, known for exemplary performance of his duties. He was also intimately familiar with the local geography, especially the bays and coves of the tideland marshes. Perhaps with his assistance we might reach Virginia, after all.

While David and I rested in the dark thicket, Robey crossed the river in a boat belonging to Jones to make arrangements in Virginia for our concealment and travel there.

Jones visited Port Tobacco and loitered in a tavern to see what information he could obtain concerning our relentless pursuers. Practically everyone there claimed to have seen me in one area or another in various disguises, even posing as a woman, and all drunkenly speculated upon their use of the reward money.

According to Jones, a Detective Williams bought several drinks, and then whispered: "I am authorized to offer one hundred thousand dollars of government money to any man who will tell me where Booth is."

From previous conversations with Jones, I had learned the man had lost almost everything he owned serving the Confederacy. The reward money was a princely sum, a temptation for the most loyal friend. But he replied without hesitation: "Well, that is a big sum, and it ought to get him if money will do it."

I had found Jones to be a man of his word, but I also knew he was not in sympathy with my deed. Therefore, I was astounded to hear he had so casually dismissed an easy fortune. His simple answer to my query shall live with me to my dying day.

"I would have had more money, but I would have lost what is worth infinitely more . . . my honor."

Now we must cross the Potomac. Jones came for us after dark with two of his own horses. He had learned that a description of the mounts David and I had rented in Washington had been circulated in this area, so we must abandon them here. Jones and Herold led the horses into a bottomless pit of quicksand, slashed their throats, and waited until they disappeared without a trace.

On their return Jones unwrapped the dressing on my leg and found the wound to be festered around a small spicule of bone protruding from the purplish skin over my ankle. This splinter must be removed.

I liberally anesthetized myself from the bottle of whiskey provided by Jones and directed David to hold my leg firmly. While I clamped my teeth on a twig and averted my eyes, Jones grasped the bone fragment with pincers, and with one jerk snatched it free. After the initial agony had subsided and I had downed several additional swallows of liquid anesthesia, I was ready to ride.

Jones and David boosted me on my horse and they mounted in tandem on theirs. During the three or four mile ride through the thicket to the Potomac shore, I continued to comfort myself from the bottle. Although my journey was thereby rendered reasonably comfortable, my temporary lack of sobriety in an attempt to ease the severe pains in my leg would result in potentially disastrous consequences this night.

I was placed in the stern to man the rudder, concealing my compass and a small candle under an old hat. Jones gave us explicit directions for landing on the Virginia shore and refused any payment for his services, silencing my protests with: "I did not do this for money. If you want to pay me eighteen dollars for the boat, that is what it cost me, but I will take no more."

I paid him the meager sum, expressed our eternal gratitude as best I could, and we shoved off into the darkness.

CHAPTER FOUR

David manned the oars with a will but could not contend with the unexpected swiftness of the current and a wind that whistled over our bow no matter which way we turned. No doubt my usually acute mental faculties had been dulled by frequent sips from the whiskey bottle, now almost empty. I could make no sense of the compass and seldom could see it, for the plagued wind blew out the candle each time I attempted a reading.

Poor David rowed all night without ceasing. At dawn he pulled into a cove to hide us. I was then able to see the compass and was close to sober, thus permitting an accurate orientation of our position. Much to my chagrin and dismay I discovered we were still in Maryland, farther from our intended landing in Virginia than when we left Jones.

With hostile cavalry patrolling the shore and Federal gunboats steaming up and down the Potomac, we had no choice but to conceal ourselves among the reeds and wait for darkness.

My exhausted companion fell immediately to sleep, crumpled like a rag doll on the floor of the boat. Before joining him in the arms of Morpheus, I reflected on the courage and stamina of this youth who I had so misjudged.

In our initial meetings prior to the events so far related, I assumed David Herold to be an immature, callow youth whose only virtue was his abject devotion to me. But in the past few days he had evidenced unstinting bravery, admirable initiative, and indefatigable concern for my welfare and the success of our venture. I had no doubt that I could not have escaped thus far without him. Certainly this noble lad deserved a far kinder fate than that which befell him.

By nightfall I had rested, my head was clear, and the pain in my leg was less. David had slept most of the day and rowed with renewed energy. The winds were calmer, and my use of the compass had improved remarkably. Early morning found us ashore in Virginia at last. We concealed our small craft by swamping it, then covering it with reeds. We had landed only a short distance from the home of a Mrs. Quesenberry, who was related to Samuel Jones and had been recommended by him as a temporary safe haven. This gracious lady supplied us with a lavish meal, complete with a tot of excellent brandy and a few hours respite from our flight. But it was essential that David and I keep moving as much as possible, so we left for the short journey to another Southern sympathizer, Dr. Richard Stuart—a name I shall never forget. His home had been a meeting place of the Confederate Secret Service during the war, and I assumed he would at least extend to us the same courtesies provided by our recent hostess.

But this coward would not venture from his home to meet us and sent out a servant with a small parcel of food and directions to the cabin of a former slave of Stuart's a quarter mile away.

In stark contrast to the compassion of Samuel Mudd, this Dr. Stuart sent a cripple and young boy on their way without so much as opening his door to them.

I struggled on my crutches, with David helping as much as he could without actually carrying me, to the freedman's shack. The Negro, William Lucas, was sorely frightened, and only the inducement of a substantial cash payment caused him to accommodate us for the night. Before I dropped into an exhausted sleep, I composed a letter to Stuart apprising him of my feelings. Although many years have passed since its composition, my rancor has not diminished, and I can recall the missive almost verbatim:

My Dear Sir,

Forgive me, but I have some pride. I cannot blame you for your lack of hospitality. You should know your own affairs best. I was sick, tired, had a broken limb, and was sorely in need of medical assistance. I would not have turned a dog away from my door in such a plight. However, you did send out something to eat for which I not only thank you, but, on account of the rebuke and manner in which it was given, I insist on making payment. It is not the substance but the way kindness is extended that makes one happy in the acceptance thereof. The sauce to the meat is ceremony. Please accept the enclosed $5.00 (although hard to spare) for what I have received.

Most respectfully, your obedient servant.

I signed it with a flourish.

With the inducement of $10.00 cash, Lucas was persuaded to hitch up his wagon and take us to Port Royal on the Rappahannock River, some sixteen miles distant. I lay headfirst in the wagon bed, and planks were laid across the side boards. An assortment of household goods belonging to Lucas was piled on top of these boards, and a crate of live chickens was tied above my feet. Lucas's young son rode atop the pile on a soiled mattress, adding to the deception of an old Negro moving to a new home, a sight not unfamiliar in those troubled times. David had ridden ahead on a borrowed mule to rendezvous with Gerald Robey and arrange a ferry across the Rappahannock.

The arduous journey was without event except for the increasing pain in my leg from the jostling wagon, the stifling compartment in which I was hidden, and the pungent soiling of my lower extremities by the infernal chickens.

Just after old Lucas said we were almost to the ferry, he suddenly exclaimed: "There them soldiers is!"

I, of course, assumed he meant Federal soldiers and resigned myself to capture and death. The crate of chickens was tossed aside, and I was dragged from my refuge. Imagine my surprise and relief when I gazed into the friendly faces of Herold and Robey.

At the ferry I was introduced to three Confederate soldiers, Major Ruggles, Captain Jett, and Lieutenant Bainbridge, who had been enlisted by Robey to assist us. Lucas immediately left with his wagon and his small son riding David's mule. Without further delay we crossed the river to its southern shore at Port Royal.

David Herold and Gerald Robey planned to leave with Captain Jett for the nearby town of Bowling Green and scout that area for the Federals. Since Dr. Mudd had cut off my left boot, that foot had been bare except for bandages. So while in town the men would purchase a pair of shoes for me. When I reached into my coat for my check book, I discovered my roll of papers was gone. It must have fallen out when I was dragged from the wagon. Inside this roll not only was my check book on a Canadian bank, but my diary, letters from a friend, pictures of my sister and other ladies—all incriminating, to say the least.

Robey promptly obtained the use of a small boat and propelled it swiftly across the river in pursuit of William Lucas to retrieve my possessions.

An immediate change in plans was necessary. Davy would remain close by the river to await Robey's return, then the two would walk to meet Captain Jett and me at Garrett's farm about three miles distant. Mr. Richard Henry Garrett was a Confederate sympathizer with a hospitable family, and the route to his farm was well known to Robey.

I was boosted onto Jett's horse behind him, and we departed for the Garretts' with Bainbridge and Ruggles serving as rear guard. Upon arrival, Jett requested accommodations for me, identifying me as a fellow soldier who had broken his leg when his horse fell. Mr. Garrett was very sympathetic to our needs, but stated he had no beds available. His two sons had recently returned from the Army, and he also had a schoolteacher boarding in his home. Jett turned his horse to ride on when Garrett's son, William, spoke up: "Papa, he can have my room, and I will sleep in the barn."

Of course, I protested this outburst of hospitality, but the gallant lad would hear no more. Soon I was resting comfortably on a soft bed, sampling a fairly respectable bottle of whiskey furnished by the Garretts. After ensuring that my immediate needs were met, Captain Jett left for Gouldman's Hotel in nearby Bowling Green where he was keeping company with one of Mr. Gouldman's daughters. Ruggles and Bainbridge made camp in the woods near the road to the Garrett's home, ready to alert us of any approaching Federal troops. Accordingly I spent my first restful night since my visit with Dr. Mudd nearly ten days past.

Breakfast was plain but nourishing, and I spent the morning resting on the porch or hobbling about the yard on my crutches, anxiously awaiting the return of David Herold and Gerald Robey with my papers.

My concern became much more acute around noon when from the piazza I spied a group of Federal troopers galloping down the road toward Bowling Green. They had barely disappeared when Bainbridge and Ruggles rode up to announce that the entire area was infested with Federal cavalry. Even more forbidding was their sighting of mounted civilians—detectives, or worse yet, vigilantes—all seeking the lucrative reward for my capture.

We could not possibly escape for long with me riding tandem with one of these men, and, too, we must go our separate ways as soon as possible. Despite my crutches, I must flee to the woods immediately until the two Confederates could find a mount for me. Once I had put some considerable distance from the Garretts' home, these men would direct Robey and David to me after they had returned with my precious papers.

I hobbled as rapidly as my condition would permit to a dense stand of trees, rested for a moment, then plunged deeper into the thicket. Sweat dripped from my brow and down my arms so that I could barely manipulate the crutches, but I pressed on. All too soon, pain and exhaustion overcame me, and I lowered myself to the forest carpet of pine needles, panting like a trapped animal, unable to move.

Unarmed and defenseless, unable to rise, I turned my head to the sound of approaching hoof beats and steeled myself for the end.

It was Ruggles and Bainbridge, with a saddled horse in tow. They helped me to mount, and we galloped west. It was now about mid-afternoon. We followed backcountry paths and headed generally southwest, pausing only briefly to rest the horses and our backsides. Approximately twenty-five miles from the Garrett farm, we stopped for a moment while I expressed my heartfelt thanks to these courageous men who had rescued me, then we went our separate ways. I never saw Ruggles or Bainbridge again, but I shall never forget that, if not for them, my life would have ended at the Garrett farm as so many have claimed.

All that night and through early morning of the following day, I pressed on through a land of undulant hills and shattered forests still infested with detritus of the recent war. Ruined wagons, caissons, endless trenches and redoubts speckled the open areas like a malignant rash upon the land.

It seemed as though the entire population was in transit. Ragged, singing Negro families moved steadily towards the north, meeting equally ragged, morose young Confederate soldiers struggling south. Fully a quarter of these battered men had lost an arm or leg, some both. They shuffled along on makeshift crutches or rode dull-eyed, emaciated mules to whatever inevitably grim future awaited them. Not a single soldier retained the strength or will to return my greetings. They plodded silently up and down the hills, following the figure in front of them like mindless insects.

Depressing as it was, I blended with this morbid traffic to avoid detection should we encounter any Federal troops. Soon, total exhaustion compelled me to stop and rest at a small farm until midday. The sympathetic owners had no food to sell but brought a dipper of cool spring water—all they had to offer.

For the rest of that day and most of that night, I journeyed farther southwest. It was obvious the full onslaught of the war had largely spared this region, and several roadside inns were open for business. I was able to purchase barely edible food, and their whiskey was hardly palatable, even for one as desperately in need of a drink as I.

As each mount became debilitated by my relentless pace, I would trade for another, and raced through the gentle hills and valleys of southwestern Virginia. Near Warfield, I crossed the Big Sandy River and entered eastern Kentucky.

Because of the long hours each day in the saddle, my leg was healing far too slowly. Riding was distinctly uncomfortable, and I walked with a pronounced limp. Two days after leaving the river, I had covered nearly sixty miles, eventually halting at a small inn maintained by the young Widow Caldwell and her ten-year-old son.

Surpassing the widow's bountiful feast served that evening was her delicate skill with which she attended my wounded leg. New wrappings and splints were applied with transcendent tenderness while she murmured touching expressions of sympathy. Before she completed her task, I had concluded that it would be propitious for me to pause for a time in this village and telegraph my bank in Canada for additional funds.

That evening I accomplished a long-overdue bath and shave, emptied a small bottle of good brandy, and enjoyed progressively more flirtatious repartée with Mrs. Caldwell followed by the luscious gratification of clean sheets and a featherbed.

Over a sumptuous breakfast served by the proprietress, I learned that her enterprising son was more than willing to run errands in town for a small sum. Without further ado, I engaged the young lad for tasks that would require his absence for the better part of that day. His mother and I became much better acquainted over the hours that followed, satisfying needs too long denied us. Her expertise, I soon learned, was not confined to the kitchen.

For the next week I did everything humanly possible to keep the athletic Mrs. Caldwell and her industrious son inordinately occupied. For generously lengthy portions of time I failed to appreciate any sensation of pain from my injured leg, but perhaps my sensory system was so suffused with pleasure it dared not admit a discordant note. I could have easily dallied for a longer idyll; however, the money had been wired from Canada and I had exhausted all plausible errands for young Master Caldwell in such a small town.

I took my leave from the voluptuous widow, affirming on bended knee my intentions to return. My performance was masterful to the degree I almost believed it myself, but I departed with a clear conscience. After all, the widow was left with a full purse, a wealth of new experience, and a son who had learned at a very tender age that one cannot earn money staying at home.

CHAPTER FIVE

"But Wilkes . . . you're dead!" the lady screeched, and swooned through her just-opened door into my arms.

Thus I was greeted at the unpretentious home of Cordelia Newman, my mother's half-sister. I had ridden almost the entire length of Kentucky during the month of May and longed for a safe respite from my travels. Although I had never met Mrs. Newman, she had followed my illustrious stage career in the newspapers, easily recognizing me from numerous published photographs. Also my dear mother had written her several times praising the performances of Father, Edwin, and me, often enclosing playbills and pictures.

I assisted Aunt Cordelia to a velvet couch in her parlor, apparently decorated in early bordello, and fanned her vigorously until she could speak. The first words from her vermilion lips fell like sweet music on this tired traveler's ears, and I knew immediately I was among blood kin.

"Brandy, for God's sake, brandy," she moaned. "It's on the sideboard."

I rested her hennaed locks on a tasseled mauve pillow and ceased my fanning. From the ornate decanter I poured a generous slug of brandy into an obviously unwashed glass and pressed it to her lips.

"God Almighty, Wilkes!" she roared with surprising vigor. "I've just seen a ghost. Fill the bloody glass."

I responded with alacrity and, being the gentleman that I am, could not permit a lady to drink alone. The medicinal effects of her draught were apparent almost immediately. Aunt Cordelia sat up, seized her fan from my grasp, and wielded it vigorously. She swallowed once and recovered her honeyed voice.

"Land sakes, my boy, you gave me such a fright. The papers all said you were killed in some barn in Virginia." She leaned toward me and whispered: "Did you really shoot Lincoln?"

I could only nod in reply, fearing her response.

Cordelia clinked her glass to mine and smiled. "Good for you, Wilkes, I never liked that old gorilla anyhow." She patted the seat beside her invitingly. "Now, fill our glasses again and come sit by your aunt. We need to talk."

The brandy and her hospitality soothed my anxiety, and I did as bidden. Two brimming tumblers were downed almost simultaneously, and we tapped our glasses in a mutual toast. Like two old friends, Aunt Cordelia and I immediately commenced that unique Southern custom, scandalous conversation, sometimes known as "cussin'an'discussin' ".

Of course, I was more than eager to hear any news she had heard or read about the assassination and its aftermath, but good manners dictated that I first inquire about events in her life. It was extremely difficult to concentrate on her narrative, for Cordelia was gowned in a shockingly low-cut frock that barely contained her ample bosoms. With each deep exhalation a tiny cloud of talcum would puff from her cleavage, and I could not help but think of a Mississippi steamer battling its way upstream.

Just before the war she had married Ambrose, a prosperous cotton broker, but they had not been blessed with children. As Aunt Cordelia so delicately expressed it: "Dear Ambrose had a big gun, bless his soul, but it only fired blanks."

Their small accumulation of wealth had vanished after Yankee sailors had blockaded the Southern ports. Cotton bales then were useless as a source of revenue and were piled on the ramparts to absorb Union bullets.

"That silly man just had to enlist"—she sighed—"and ended up dyin' of typhoid somewhere near Mobile." She sponged a tear from her brightly rouged cheek. "I don't even know where he's buried, poor thing. All I had left was this house . . . and these." She sighed and gazed down demurely at her Brobdingnagian breasts. An aromatic nebula of scented powder erupted from her bodice. "So I went into business for myself." Cordelia smiled coyly. "And I've done right well, too."

I gratefully accepted her offer to "stay here as long as you like, honey," and was shown to a back bedroom. While I soaked away the accumulated grime in a sudsy hot tub and shaved, a servant was dispatched to purchase newspapers which I could peruse at leisure. Aunt Cordelia would be engaged for the remainder of the day and evening, "takin' care of business, honey."

LINCOLN'S ASSASSIN DEAD
CONSPIRATORS JAILED

I read and re-read the newspaper accounts while my emotions ebbed and flowed like a raging ocean. Sorrow, anger, amazement, and shocked disbelief washed over me until I was too weak to read more. How could our plans have been so misconstrued? How could so many innocents suffer? How had the guilty escaped? From whence had come these traitorous lies, perjury, and slander?

The accounts raved on of our conspiracy and the accused conspirators. Did no one realize a much greater conspiracy was even now being foisted on a gullible and believing populace? My first impulse was to seek out a prominent newsman and relate the true story as I alone knew it. But who would believe me, a dead man? And who was the imposter, the man in the barn, the false John Wilkes Booth?

I spread the scandalous accounts about the room and fortified myself with liberal doses of Cordelia's excellent brandy. Then I set about systematically to analyze the perfidious narratives and glean some insight into events since my hasty departure from Virginia.

The lies, intrigue, and betrayals sickened me. Of our original band, only John Surratt remained at large. The innocent as well as the guilty were incarcerated under vile and inhuman conditions awaiting trial which was sure to be a farce. Paine had hacked Seward and stabbed Seward's son, but failed to kill anyone. The dolt had been promptly arrested at Mary Surratt's. This innocent lady was jailed as was the guiltless Dr. Mudd. Atzerodt, whose only crimes were drunkenness and incompetence, who had not even attempted his assignment, was swept into the net. Michael O'Laughlin and Ned Spangler, the latter having done no more than hold my horse for me at Ford's Theatre, were confined with the others.

And poor, poor Herold, my David, my loyal companion, had been brutally dragged from a burning barn at the Garretts', tied to a tree, and threatened with immediate hanging. This lovely lad, who prayed daily and whose adoration of me would melt a marble statue's heart, was vilified as some sort of monster. Now he waited, hooded, frightened and alone, in a cell while the Yankee press clamored for his summary execution.

From the often conflicting newspaper accounts of events

following Lincoln's death, I was able to construct a plausible scenario involving those who had pursued me.

At Surratt's Tavern the old handyman, John Lloyd, was strung up by his thumbs and deprived of alcohol for forty-eight hours. The latter punishment represented inhuman cruelty to one of Lloyd's ilk, and he soon admitted that he had directed David and me to Dr. Mudd's home. The doctor maintained that he had never recognized me but did admit to treating my leg. Several witnesses confirmed our crossing of the Potomac into Virginia and our subsequent movements there.

William Rollins, ferryman at the Rappahannock River, identified a picture of me and informed the troopers that I had ridden off in the company of a Confederate soldier named Jett.

Captain Jett was captured at Gouldman's Hotel in Bowling Green, and, with a pistol pressed to his head, confessed he had directed us to Garretts' farm.

In the dead of night, Union cavalry had surrounded the house and outbuildings, then dragged the elderly Mr. Garrett from his bed. When told to produce the men he was harboring, and unaware of David and Robey in his barn, Garrett answered truthfully, referring to the soldiers and me: "They've gone to the woods."

This failed to satisfy his interrogators. They produced a rope and threatened to string him up immediately, in full view of his terrified wife and children. His panic-stricken young son, William, screamed: "Two men are in the barn!"

The building was surrounded, and demands made for the occupants' surrender. The newspaper accounts of dialogue which allegedly followed were so disgustingly melodramatic and obviously contrived they are not worthy of repetition here. Suffice it to say that even in my younger inexperienced days as an actor, I would have refused any rôle requiring the utterance of such drivel.

In any event, David Herold capitulated. The terrified young man was snatched from the building and shackled to a tree, then the barn was set afire to flush out his recalcitrant companion.

A shot rang out. Almost every newspaper attributed the fatal bullet to a different source—General Conger, Luther Baker, suicide, or a Sergeant Boston Corbett.

A dying man was dragged from the conflagration, mortally wounded in the neck. More pathetically written dialogue attributed to the victim followed—cries of "Mother, forgive me," and "Useless, useless." No doubt such literary fantasies issued from the pen of a witless copy editor who further desecrated a tragic, useless death.

Why Gerald Robey, for it could have been none other than he in the barn with David Herold, chose not to surrender mystifies me to this day. I can only speculate that he preferred the immediate effects of a bullet (possibly by his own hand) to prison and certain execution by hanging.

Robey in no way resembles me, so the cover-up conspiracy begins immediately. I can easily imagine the panic and frustration which must have gripped the officers and detectives present when they realized the wrong man was dead, and I, Booth, had escaped.

However, found in Robey's clothing was the packet he was returning to me containing my diary, pictures, and personal items. This packet was the sole evidence for identifying Robey's body as mine.

The desperation to conceal this monstrous subterfuge can easily be surmised from endless newspaper accounts of persons summoned to certify that the dead man was indeed John Wilkes Booth. Sworn affidavits were obtained from officers and troopers, all Union, at the scene, witnesses and government officials, all Union, who viewed the body later, and doctors, all Union, who performed the autopsy.

And what became of the body? Some reported it was buried at night on an island in the Potomac marshes, some swore it was sewn into a canvas shroud with cannon balls and dumped into the Potomac River, and others averred it was buried in the Washington Arsenal Penitentiary.

It certainly goes without saying that, because of my illustrious career in the public eye, literally thousands of reliable witnesses could have easily identified me on sight. But not one personal friend, family member, fellow performer, bartender, or those arrested as my accomplices were asked to view the body. Only witnesses hand-picked by the Federal government were quoted, many obviously hoping to share in the reward purse of over $200,000.

It should be obvious to the most casual reader of these accounts that high officials in the new government regime wished to bring the matter of Lincoln's assassination to a swift and final conclusion. Public outrage must be calmed and curiosity suppressed. "Booth's" death, followed by severe punishment of his conspirators would accomplish this end.

Certainly the worthy gentlemen now in charge of the newly United States would abhor an investigation that might reveal their Great Conspiracy. I feared that none of those jailed and accused of being an associate of mine would survive the wrath of such evil men.

The unkindest cut of all awaited me in a letter to a New York paper authored by my brother Edwin. Even prior to the war our sympathies were diametrically opposite, but in more recent years Edwin's and my political differences became so acerbic that our sister banned any discussions of the subject under her roof.

By happenstance, some years past, Edwin had rescued Lincoln's son, Robert, from being trampled by a carriage in Jersey City. In appreciation, the President had invited Edwin to give a private performance of *Richard III* for him, Mrs. Lincoln, and distinguished guests. Needless to say, Edwin had been a devoted follower of Lincoln and his minions since. But I felt a deep sense of betrayal and abandonment as I read:

April 20, 1865
To the People of the United States
My Fellow Citizens,

When a nation is overwhelmed with sorrow by a great public calamity, the mention of private grief would under ordinary circumstances be an intrusion, but under those by which I am surrounded, I feel sure that a word from me will not be so regarded by you.

It has pleased God to lay at the door of my afflicted family the lifeblood of our great, good, and martyred President. Prostrated to the very earth by this dreadful event, I am yet but too sensible that other mourners fill the land. To them, to you, one and all go forth our deep unutterable sympathy, our abhorrence and devastation of this most foul and atrocious of crimes.

For my mother and sister, for the two remaining brothers, and my own poor self, there is nothing to be said except that we are placed without any agency of our own. For our loyalty as dutiful though humble citizens, as well as for our consistent and, as we had some reason to believe, successful efforts to elevate our name, personally and professionally, we appeal to the record of the past. For our present position we are not responsible. For the future, alas! I shall struggle on in my retirement, with a heavy heart, an oppressed memory, and a wounded name—dreadful burdens—to my welcome grave.

Your afflicted friend,
Edwin Booth

I wondered if Edwin believed the stories of my death, or worse, if he even cared. Profoundly vexed by these published canards, I crumpled the entire pile of newspapers into a wad and consigned them to the kitchen stove. A stiff jolt of brandy rapidly exerted its desired medicinal effects, and I immersed my thoughts into preparations for my departure the following morn.

My journey would take me further south into Mississippi to visit friends I could trust, then probably downriver to New Orleans and a sea voyage to follow.

Such pleasant images were abruptly split asunder like summer lightning cleaves a pine. I jerked erect as a horrendous realization intruded my thoughts. They will come looking for me.

Foolishly I had relaxed after reading of poor Robey's death in my stead. It would be an unmitigated disaster and monumentally stupid for anyone in official Washington to admit that John Wilkes Booth lived. But those of the Great Conspiracy, whose leader, the infamous Z, was now President, would know that I was alive, posing an unacceptable risk. They would have to eliminate the possibility that Booth would ever appear. Now I would be the hunted, the target of an assassin.

I must leave for Mississippi tonight.

BOOK TWO

He mounts the storm, and walks upon the wind.

"An Essay on Man"
Alexander Pope

CHAPTER SIX

"Well, old buddy, you were right as usual," I admitted, flopping into a comfortable recliner surrounded by walls of books in Ken's cozy study. "This business with Booth's supposed journal has really opened a can of worms for me."

"How's that?" Ken sighed, reluctantly shutting down his word processor and work on his latest romance novel. "I thought you were really gung ho on all your research about that assassin."

"I was. I still am. But I thought all this stuff about Booth and his mummy was a dead issue. Oh, I am sorry, no pun intended," I apologized as Ken's eyes rolled heavenward.

"For example, I punched in 'John Wilkes Booth' on the Internet and nearly thirty-five thousand entries appeared. Books on the subject published as recently as two or three years ago came up . . . stage plays, FBI investigations of Booth's boot, endless scholarly dissertations, even a comparison of John Wilkes with Monica Lewinsky."

"Aw, come on, Pres. Be serious." Ken grinned and shook his head.

"No, really. There was even an ad for a John Wilkes kissing booth."

"Oh, please," Ken moaned. "Haven't you found anything pertinent? Remember, you volunteered to do the legwork on this project. Do you think the journal's authentic or not? I don't want to waste our time on some side-show hoax."

"Honestly, Ken, the more I read, the more confused I

65

become. But what I've discovered so far convinces me of one thing. The government's investigation of events preceding and following Lincoln's assassination was the most inept probe in our nation's history. What a cast of sleazy characters and incompetents. No wonder so many conflicting conspiracy theories and stories of Booth's escape abound."

"Do you think Booth escaped the burning barn?" Ken asked, cutting directly to the nucleus of the matter as was typical of him.

I tilted forward in the chair and frowned for a moment before answering.

"Back in high school when I first researched the subject, and up until recently, I was completely convinced the history books were correct. Booth was shot and killed by a Sergeant Boston Corbett in a burning barn at the Garrett farm on April Twenty-Sixth, Eighteen Sixty-Five. I just re-read Jim Bishop's Nineteen Fifty-Five book, *The Day Lincoln Was Shot*, and he says. . . ." I pulled a notepad from my back pocket and read. " 'For years afterward there were stories that it wasn't Booth who was shot, but the stories were wrong. It was Booth and, years later, when the government removed his body from under a stone floor in a prison, and sent it home, the Booth family identified the remains as those of John Wilkes Booth and buried him in the family plot.' "

I looked at Ken with a smile.

"So," he said. "Why the grin? That story's pretty convincing. And with Booth dead, our journal's obviously a fake"

"But what if Booth wasn't killed in the barn, and his family knew that. Wouldn't they claim the body was John Wilkes? To do otherwise would expose a monumental conspiracy and force the government to find Booth and bring him to justice . . . or, far more likely, 'disappear' him before further damage was done? He'd be safe if everyone was convinced he was dead. Don't forget, there was no DNA testing back then."

"But Edwin, his brother, practically disowned him in that letter," Ken said. "Why would he lie and say the body was John Wilkes if it wasn't?"

"Because as best I can determine, Edwin based his identification on the word of Wilkes's dentist, an old family friend of the Booths and a particularly close friend of Wilkes's mother."

I stood up abruptly and began pacing as if testifying in a courtroom, then paused and smiled down at Ken.

"Based on what all I've been perusing lately, and in the light of present-day medical knowledge, psychiatrists would have a field day exploring the relationship between John Wilkes and his mother. He adored her, and she doted on him. I'm convinced she would say or do anything to save her son, and what's more would convince, or order, any family member or close friend of the Booths to follow suit."

Ken whistled softly, then murmured: "By God, Pres, I think you just might be on to something."

"That's just a theory I'm working on so far, but I've found a treasure trove of information right here in good old San Angelo."

"Now don't tell me Booth ended up in our fair city."

"No, but listen to this. Many years ago I had a patient, Judge Emsy Swaim, from the town of Eden, just southeast of us. He was convinced Booth had escaped and lived for a time in Texas. To support his claim, Judge Swaim had amassed one of the world's largest collections of affidavits from witnesses who supposedly knew Booth after Eighteen

Sixty-Five. The judge willed his entire collection to the West Texas Collection at our university library here. Yesterday I called Suzanne Campbell at the library, who has catalogued all this material, and I plan to start poring through the stuff today." I smiled sheepishly. "I guess I just wanted you to tell me I'm not wasting our time."

"Go for it," Ken said. "Now you won't think I'm foolish when I tell you I've already sent a sample page of the journal to some old FBI friends in Washington to see if the paper can be dated, and maybe get some clues from the handwriting. Unfortunately some of the pages, particularly around the mid-portion, are fragmented and almost illegible. I sealed the worst ones in a packet and sent them along, too. Maybe the technicians there can decipher some of it. I still haven't heard anything about the mummy's DNA. So while we're waiting, why don't you press on with your research?" He turned back to his word processor. "But right now I've got to save another fair damsel from the clutches of an evil villain."

CHAPTER SEVEN

My anxiety and the almost overpowering need for haste were overshadowed by the tenderness and genuine affection I felt for Aunt Cordelia. This genteel lady, shunned by so-called polite society, had welcomed me, a true outcast, in time of need, and asked nothing in return.

When she engulfed me in an energetic and aromatic embrace of farewell, I was almost moved to tears. Only my superb thespian skills allowed me to control my voice and emotions as I bade her farewell.

"May God be with you, Wilkes," she whispered. "You stay safe and come back to see me, hear?"

To this day the scent of talcum or the aroma of good brandy awake memories of dear Aunt Cordelia and her heart of pure gold.

It was but a brief and uncomfortable journey by coach to Paducah, and there I booked passage on a stern-wheeler hauling cotton to New Orleans. At the ticket office and again at the dock, I behaved in a most ungentlemanly and boorish fashion ensuring that I would be remembered. I had no intention of completing the trip and would abandon the vessel at the most propitious time, thereby confusing any possible pursuers. Aunt Cordelia had already given me the name and address of a family residing near the river in Mississippi who would shelter me until I decided upon my final destination.

The next two days were spent in idle relaxation, for I felt relatively safe from pursuit and my leg was much improved.

The time proved very lucrative, for the few passengers and some of the crew insisted upon repeated attempts to recoup their initial losses in a game of poker. Fools never learn that bluff is no substitute for brains. I did not even find cheating necessary to fleece those sheep.

Feigning illness, I retired to my cabin, then departed the vessel during a pre-dawn stop for fuel. For a small sum from my poker winnings, I paid one of the woodcutters to transport me a short distance to Beloit City, Mississippi, and the home of Aunt Cordelia's friends, the J. C. Burrus family.

The Burrus residence was well known as a haven for Confederate soldiers returning to their homes in Texas and beyond. Many of these men were traveling to join with General Shelby and his troopers who would cross the Río Grande into Mexico and on into Central America. These brave men and their officers had refused to surrender after Appomattox, and large rewards were posted by the Federal government for their capture. Not one Confederate soldier had ever been betrayed while at the Burrus home, and any true Southerner was always welcome.

While aboard the stern-wheeler I remained clean-shaven and had cropped my trademark raven hair even shorter. Recalling our captain's last name as Lamar, I introduced myself to my new hosts as Mr. L.A. Marr—"Call me Lawrence."—and expressed an interest in purchasing real estate around their thriving community.

The room I rented was extremely well appointed and kept scrupulously clean by a comely lass of fifteen years, possibly less. Naturally in less than a day the poor thing was totally enraptured with me. Since she was employed by my hosts, I initially feigned disinterest, but the fresh flowers and sweetly suggestive notes left daily in my room began to weaken my resolve. Surely it was far better, I reasoned, for a cultured gentleman such as I to introduce this willing girl to the keys of heaven, than some untutored brutish lout far less likely to appreciate her finer qualities.

For the next week my days were spent riding about the countryside with Mr. Burrus, affecting an interest in local property. My nights were consumed with tutoring my eager student. She was an apt pupil, performing her lessons with enthusiasm and increasing skill.

But I must move on. I could not shake the feeling that something was gaining on me. In my conversations with the locals, I emphasized my intention to journey on to Texas and join General Shelby or General Canby's foray onto Mexico. But I secretly booked passage on a steamer bound for St. Louis to further confuse any pursuers.

My need for haste mercifully shortened the tearful entreaties of my young companion, and she was silenced only by my solemn vow to return for her as soon as possible.

Comfortably ensconced in my stateroom, I was soon lulled into a pleasant torpor by my evening tot of brandy and the rhythmic puffing of the engine.

The door burst open with a crash!

Before I could rise, the sobbing girl flung herself into my arms, begging to be taken with me. She had obviously followed me to the landing and hidden aboard the vessel. A most awkward scene followed. I attempted to reason with the hysterical *demoiselle,* but her ears were closed. Nothing I could say would calm her. Abruptly she turned and dashed through the open door. Before I could stop her, the nymphet stumbled over the deck rail and disappeared under the churning paddle wheel.

Poor thing. I would have taken her with me—for a time. Strange, as I pen this, I do not recall the child's name.

The remainder of my voyage was uneventful; nay, it was rather tedious. No one seemed interested in a friendly game of cards, and conversation with my semi-literate and doltish fellow passengers bored me to exasperation. I spent much of the time in my room reading or perambulating about the decks to obtain a whiff of fresh air. My leg was now much less painful, although I walked with a rather stylish limp using the silver-headed cane I had purchased. Many clucks of sympathy and soothing words for the "poor man" issued from my fellow passengers as I passed, for no doubt they assumed I was recovering from war wounds. I did nothing to alter their misconception.

During our fuel stop in Memphis, I located a costumer's establishment and fashioned a detailed make-up kit to my specifications. For much of the time after we resumed our voyage, I practiced various disguises and voices to use as the occasion would demand. Now my trackers would find me a most elusive and chameleon-like quarry.

Immediately upon arriving in St. Louis, I took a room at a quiet, unimposing inn near the river, then changed my clothes and my appearance substantially with the aid of wig and moustache. Affecting a British accent, I booked passage the next day on a steam packet up the Missouri River to Kansas City. The presence of a contingent of Federal troops on board *en route* to posts in the far Northwest caused me no concern, merely enhancing my performance as a "veddy British" gentleman journeying to hunt the "wooly beasts you chaps refer to as buffalo."

Another overnight change in character was spent in Kansas City, then, I boarded a flatboat bound upriver disguised as a wounded soldier returning to his farm near Omaha. But I left the plodding vessel during its stop in Nebraska City and soon had obtained employment as a menial wagon driver in a caravan headed for Salt Lake City.

During my travels over a period of several months, I had endured the monumental discomforts and indignities of inferior steeds with pathetic saddles, rickety buggies, and throbbing steamboats. But nothing could compare with the relentless teeth-jarring pounding and stultifying boredom of a loaded freight wagon, coupled with the unavoidable campfire companionship of persons possessing the intellect and social graces of barnyard animals. I suffered an immediate longing, unfortunately never fulfilled for the entire trip, for conversation unrelated to animal lust and bodily functions.

I had hoped to obtain some relief from my boredom by perusing a bundle of newspapers prepared by the hotel's concierge prior to my departure, but the first one I chose depressed me beyond measure.

Under a rotogravure drawing of four cocooned bodies dangling from a rude scaffold like strange fruit was an insensitive story detailing the summary trial and execution of my former companions. Paine (who they called Powell), Atzerodt, poor, innocent Mary Surratt, and David, that dear boy, had been hanged on July 7th in full view of over 1,000 pitiless gawkers. Their last sight on this earth was the open graves which awaited them. Then they were hooded and strung up like chickens.

The remainder of the article described their death throes and gleeful comments of morbid spectators in sickening detail. I could read no more of this atrocity.

Michael O'Laughlin, Samuel Arnold, and even Dr. Mudd were sentenced to long prison terms. Only John Surratt had escaped, and a worldwide search for him was in progress.

One brief account speculated at length about the site of my interment. My body was variously reported as being at the bottom of the Potomac, in the old Washington Arsenal, or dissolved in quicklime. Certainly the Great Conspiracy and Z would ensure that my supposed remains, wherever they might be, would not be located soon.

In all honesty, and as a gentleman of honor, I must admit my guilt as the sole murderer in all this tangled web of lies and deceit. But in no account of the so-called trial was there mention that our purpose was to kidnap, not kill, President Lincoln, until so ordered by the traitorous Z.

Paine was certainly guilty of assault, but not murder. Seward lived. Dr. Mudd and Mary Surratt are innocent of any crime. To execute her was murder, pure and simple. Atzerodt was guilty only of drunkenness and incompetence. If these be crimes worthy of hanging, a sufficient number of gallows could not be built to accommodate guilty politicians alone.

And poor David Herold, hanged for the crime of loyalty to his tarnished hero, nothing more. O'Laughlin, Arnold, and Spangler were confined with Dr. Mudd to a remote dank prison in the Florida Keys on nebulous charges.

Certainly even the most ignorant reader of these newspaper accounts could discern the true motive behind such unjust sentences by a biased tribunal. The unfortunate victims were silenced quickly so that no one could reveal the inescapable fact that I, the only murderer, had eluded their grasp. The barely contained anger, fear, and frustration consuming the Great Conspiracy were wreaked upon my hapless friends by perfidious officials.

Theirs is the greater crime. They are the murderers.

That night I consigned the remainder of my packet to the campfire. Even as the newspaper articles burned, they reflected more heat than light.

While I gazed into the dwindling flames, an unfamiliar name from one of the paper's accounts recurred like an unbidden melody into my reflections. Whippet Nilgai, an Indian scout possessing an uncanny ability to track fugitives, had been employed for a time by Federal troops and detectives pursuing me through Maryland and Virginia. Was it his peculiar name that compelled me to recall it, or was some atavistic sixth sense of mine portending danger from this mysterious source?

To an enterprising young farmer or cattleman the Nebraska plains may have beckoned as paradise on earth, but I found the terrain to be an endless succession of featureless prairies, deep cold rivers, and yawning expanses of nothingness. The water of their rivers was brackish and often laced with alkali, barely palatable even after boiling. It was certainly unfit to mix with the small cache of whiskey hidden in my bags. But this created no problem for me. I have always averred in respect to mixing whiskey with water: "Good whiskey does not need it, and bad whiskey does not deserve it."

I yearned for the bustle and excitement of cities and ached with the frustration of a skilled performer who has no stage. To pass the time I recited long passages of Shakespearian dialogue to the rear-ends of my mules, with little effort imagining them to be pithy drama critics of my past acquaintance.

One evening at the campfire, out of sheer boredom, I stood and declaimed a brief soliloquy from *Richard III*. The novelty of my efforts, if nothing else, should have provoked some manner of response from the assembly. But the dullards sat gap-mouthed, slowly chewing their infernal cuds of red beans, then returned to the important business of ingesting the pathetic contents of their plates. Perhaps they thought I was a "fancy boy" craving attention, but I suspect these bovine dolts could not think at all.

I consoled myself that such companions served as excellent camouflage, for no one searching for me could ever imagine my association with such uncouth and vile-smelling ruffians. I would even have preferred the company of slaves.

As the weeks and months ground interminably past, we changed cargo, wagons, and personnel at intervening destinations, but the tedium of each day passed with the shuffling pace of an errant schoolboy returning home to certain punishment.

When we entered the stark unending landscape of Utah Territory, I could endure no more. Without so much as a farewell or request for pay, I abandoned further torture in the dead of night and joined a crew of surveyors traveling to Salt Lake City. Their enthusiasm for being a part of the pending construction of a transcontinental railroad was infectious, and their conversational level was infinitely superior to my half-witted associates of previous weeks. At last some sophisticated discourse was possible, and my spirits were elevated accordingly.

Except for drovers and rodmen of the party, this group was composed of educated gentlemen who performed their daily tasks with skill and enthusiasm. They slept in commodious tents, bathed regularly when conditions permitted, and greeted the spectacular sunsets with full stomachs and post-prandial libations of excellent whiskey. At last, civilization had arrived in this god-forsaken land.

I was sorely tempted to entertain my hosts with dramatic renditions but was cautious enough to continue my rôle as a prosperous wounded Confederate veteran bent on exploring newer opportunities in California. The weeks with these men raced by like a pleasant moveable feast. There was only one minor disruption.

One evening we were joined by a troop of Federal cavalry exploring supply routes to forts farther west. Their leader, a General Augur, was adding to our merriment with a rather ribald tale when I suddenly remembered where I had heard his name. He was the commander of troops in and around Washington who chased me into Virginia. He, of course, could not have recognized me, but I did experience some unease until he and his soldiers departed. It would have been interesting to see his reaction should he ever learn he had dined with his quarry.

CHAPTER EIGHT

It was with a feeling of deep regret that I took leave from my companions of the past months, for I knew my way ahead would be long and lonely. Spring thaws were weeks away, and the snow-bound passes through the Rocky Mountains remained closed. I must therefore follow a more southern route into California, then north through the valleys to San Francisco. The surveyors would remain in Salt Lake City until they could complete their explorations through the mountains to Reno, Sacramento, and beyond.

Although I continued to feel betrayed by Edwin's published remarks, I yearned for some contact with the family, particularly my dear mother. Had she believed the conflicting newspaper accounts of my death, or did she hold some hope that I had escaped? The telegraph would be the safest and most expeditious means of communication, but I must conceal the message and my identity from any suspicious telegrapher. At the same time it would be necessary for me to include something in the communication that would convince my mother it was authentic.

During my early childhood in Maryland, a wizened old Gypsy from a passing caravan had read my palm. At first glance the ancient crone gasped and dropped my hand, then averted her eyes and predicted a short but famous life with much tragedy. This reading had become a family joke as I rose in prominence in the theatre, particularly as a featured tragedian in works of Shakespeare. Mother would certainly recognize a reference to this episode and easily identify the sender. I also included cryptic instructions for her to meet me at a specified hotel in San Francisco three months hence and emphasized the necessity of keeping our contact completely secret for her sake as well as mine. No return address or request for a reply was given, for not until I was out of the country would I feel truly safe from the wrath of Z and his collaborators. An additional message was transmitted to the Canadian bank effecting withdrawal of sufficient funds to replenish my dwindling reserve.

The seemingly endless journey through Nevada and Arizona Territories was tedious beyond description, an unending succession of bad roads, atrocious food, unpalatable whiskey, and boring conversation. Northward through California only the roads improved.

But at last I reached San Francisco and its majestic harbor. This jewel of a city in its pristine setting and its fascinating inhabitants more than compensated for the arduous journey.

I obtained lodging in an inconspicuous but comfortable boarding house overlooking the sumptuous bay, teeming with ships. There I assumed the persona of Professor Augustin Ravenwood, tutor for children of the rich and famous, presently performing linguistic research for a prestigious New England university. This rôle allowed me to keep erratic hours, speak eloquently, dress elegantly, and conduct myself with long-postponed grandeur.

Excellent whiskey was readily available throughout this enticing city, but no more so than attractive, compliant ladies, and I devoted myself with accustomed intensity to generous samplings of each. My female acquaintances were a polyglot mixture of origins, colors, and accents, and all too soon I required a measure of self-imposed rationing to avoid total exhaustion.

The inhabitants of this exquisite metropolis introduced me to attitudes and moral values delightfully foreign to one such as I reared on the East Coast. I could only attribute their unique behavior to the fact that their moon always rose on the wrong side of the beach, somehow affecting the tidal surges of their emotional development.

For some unfathomable reason, I felt safe here. The horrific events and laborious travels of the past year were but fading memories, lavaged from my conscious being by my animated pursuit of sybaritic pleasures.

After my reunion with Mother, I planned to set sail for parts yet unknown, remaining out of the now United States for an extended time. I had taken great pains in my journey thus far to conceal my identity and purposely followed a very erratic route west, rendering it virtually impossible for anyone to trail me. I remained clean shaven and cropped my hair short. My telltale limp had all but disappeared. In no way did I now resemble the tintype and stage portraits of me that had been reproduced in newspapers. Even my own family would find it difficult to recognize me.

Over a year had passed since Lincoln's death, and all of the alleged conspirators were imprisoned or dead except John Surratt. He had apparently escaped to Europe. Lincoln's death and events that followed were no longer news. Federal troops, having completed their ravage of the South, were now engaged in a campaign designed to exterminate the pesky Indians of the plains and seize their land. Settlers were moving West, railroads were coming, and nothing would impede the self-assumed manifest destiny of greedy politicians. When I set sail, I would not regret leaving such mendacity behind me.

My eminently successful stage career and prescient oil investments in Pennsylvania, to say nothing of the sums deposited in my Canadian bank by the Confederate conspirators, had provided me with considerable wealth. I had no desire to return to the wife and children I had been forced to abandon, and who by now were surely convinced I was dead. But I longed with all my heart to embrace my dear mother one last time before my travels to begin a new life and identity.

The weeks sped by. With the excellent cuisine provided by my hosts and rambling daily walks along the exquisite bay, my health and stamina rapidly improved. I had purchased an extensive wardrobe and accouterments, in addition to new luggage and a trunk full of books for my proposed journey. In the evenings I denied myself nothing that money could buy. In spite of this extravagance, my purse actually increased from winnings at the gambling tables. It appeared that I was lucky at cards and at love—or rather at lust, to be truthful.

Since I had no way of knowing the exact date of Mother's arrival, in the evenings I began to frequent the hotel of our assignation. Soon Professor Ravenwood was a welcome visitor, known equally well for his generous tips, lovely companions, and unparalleled skill at poker. The obsequious desk clerk was well rewarded in advance for his vow to inform me secretly when a certain "mature lady from Baltimore" had arrived. Imagine his shock and disbelief had he learned that the lady I so eagerly awaited was my mother.

I was whistling with pleasure during my morning stroll when I was almost struck to my knees by the abrupt thunderclap of an ominous thought. How could I have been so stupid? After all my careful changes of identity, erratic routes, and exhausting travels, I had committed a most perfidious blunder.

Z and his minions would soon realize that my skills at disguise and experience as a noted actor would render any pursuit of me as futile. So they would surreptitiously circle my family and close friends like hawks waiting for me to contact someone, then they would follow that person and pounce. I must be eliminated very discreetly; otherwise, their ruse of my death in the barn would be exposed.

Even if they had managed to track the withdrawal of funds from my Canadian bank, that trail would lead them only as far as Salt Lake City. But now, unwittingly, I had placed the life of my beloved mother in peril. Surely the schemers would not murder her along with me. Such an event would create too much unwanted publicity. But an "accident" could easily be arranged before she revealed that she had seen her son and accounts of his death were a conspiracy of lies.

I hatched a desperate plan. Everything must be done in stealth. I must identify my mother's tracker before he learned who I was and get rid of him without endangering Mother. Firearms were out of the question. The hotel did not allow them on the premises and employed a plain-clothes policeman to monitor our card games. Participants and spectators were subjected to search before admission to the gambling lounge and were required to stay in the lounge until the evening's play had ended. A gentlemen's room opened into the lounge.

Each evening, at cards, I would carefully observe the spectators in order to recognize any new faces. One afternoon I arrived early and unshaven, complaining that no hot water was available at my lodgings. I was granted (after a substantial tip) use of the gentlemen's room, and after I had completed my ablutions, concealed my straight razor behind the mirror.

Two nights later the desk clerk whispered that the "lady from Baltimore, a Missus Boswell, has checked into Room Two Forty with her young son." She must have brought my brother Joseph. Now I must protect them both.

For the first night in some time, I lost money at poker, being intent on searching the faces of our spectators. Halfway through the evening, I noted an unfamiliar arrival. A short, muscular, swarthy individual with piercing blue eyes and lank coal-black hair took his seat well in the back of our room. Far from being as skilled an actor as I, it was obvious to me he was not there to observe the game but was searching the assembled gathering for someone.

When I saw him walk toward the men's room, I excused myself from the game and followed him. While we attended to our needs, I attempted a friendly conversation but was answered only in heavily accented monosyllables. Back at the table, I almost misplayed my hand when the stranger's name popped into my brain. Surely he was Whippet Nilgai, the Indian tracker employed by Federal troops chasing me in Maryland.

He had followed Mother here and was waiting for her to lead him to me. But I was equally sure he had not recognized me, for he departed the lounge after watching only a few more hands. I remained at the table until the end of the game to avoid suspicion, then returned to my lodging and packed all my belongings.

After a hearty breakfast I booked passage on a ship bound for the Sandwich Islands one week hence and arranged for my baggage, except for a small suitcase of necessary items, to be transferred aboard the vessel. I settled my bill with the landlord and withdrew funds from the bank. For the rest of the day, I enjoyed my last stroll around the harbor, pausing at a milliner's shop for one last item which

I concealed under the lapel of my coat.

The day was picture perfect, warm and sunny with a cool breeze blowing from the bay. My only regret was not being able to contact Mother who I knew was anxiously awaiting me, but I also knew she was being watched. At least she had young Joseph with her for companionship.

Immediately upon entering the hotel lobby, I spied Nilgai seated by the entry to the poker lounge, partially concealed by a newspaper he pretended to read. The game had not yet begun and chips were being distributed as I walked toward the open door, ignoring Nilgai's intent stare.

"Oh, Wilkes, is it really you?" The voice came from behind me. I turned and was enveloped into the loving arms of my dear mother.

While she held me close, I managed to turn us so I could watch Nilgai over her shoulder, then thrust her gently away from me and bowed.

"Madame, you have mistaken me for someone else." I smiled wickedly. "But please convey to him my compliments. He is a very fortunate man. I am Professor Augustin Ravenwood at your service."

Before she could reply, I strode through the lounge door and into the men's room. It was the greatest and most heart-breaking performance of my career. I can never erase from my mind the stricken look on Mother's face as I left her standing dejectedly in the lobby, her hopes dashed. Joseph had immediately taken her arm and spoken soothingly: "Come, Mother, let us go upstairs."

Nilgai followed me as I knew he would, still unsure of his quarry. I pretended to be occupied at the receptacle, and, as he followed suit, I stepped behind him and clasped my left hand over his mouth. Before he could struggle, I extracted the object from my lapel and plunged a nine-inch hat pin to the hilt in his right ear. As he moaned and twitched on the floor, I removed my razor from its hiding place and slashed the assassin's neck repeatedly until his head was almost severed.

I wiped the blood from my shoes and returned to my usual seat at the gaming table. My winning ways continued until a shriek from someone who had entered the men's room put an end to the game. In the confusion that followed, I strolled casually through the lobby and up the stairs to Mother's room.

I was not in the least upset over dispatching Nilgai. After all, it was self-defense. But the disappointment of my poor mother and my cold rejection of her, albeit a necessary performance, tore at my very being.

Joseph cracked the door in response to my tap and, of course, with my altered appearance, did not recognize me. When I identified myself, he swept me into the room quickly and locked the door. Mother almost swooned, then collapsed on my shoulder murmuring: "I knew it was you, Wilkes . . . I knew it was you."

We babbled excitedly for several minutes before regaining our composure. It was then necessary to discuss family matters and events of the past year. I had wreaked great sorrow on my innocent family, but Mother silenced my attempts to apologize and insisted that we press on with plans for the future.

Naturally I did not wish to distress Joseph and Mother with recent events downstairs but did relay to them my concern that agents of the government were probably searching for me, necessitating an immediate change in disguise and lodgings. I would wear Joseph's clothes to exit this hotel and rent accommodations in a rooming house only a few blocks away.

Because of my demanding career and clandestine activities in the service of our beloved Confederacy, I had not seen Joseph in a number of years. As the youngest of her offspring, he had been fawned over by Mother since early childhood. Now his voice and demeanor were far from manly, and I did not relish wearing his somewhat gaudy suits trimmed with entirely too much velvet and lace for my tastes.

But in Mother's presence, Joseph seemed genuinely glad to see me and graciously agreed to my selections from his wardrobe. In fact, he volunteered to retrieve my suitcase from the boarding house. Professor Ravenwood, he would say, had suddenly been called to an academic position out of the state. Naturally the good professor would never be seen again.

I thought it would please Mother that I would portray the rôle of her son, the priest, recently returned from Europe. She avowed with great pleasure that my authentic British accent caused her to reprise fond memories of her days as a young flower girl in London before she met Father.

For the next several days, Mother, Joseph, and I toured the city like giddy sightseers. Operas, plays, the finest restaurants, sailing the bay—nothing escaped our pursuit of pleasure. Mother seemed to possess more energy than her handsome sons, and we three basked in the envious stares of those around us. My brother's flamboyant dress and mannerisms were not unusual in this city, and, of course, everyone was deferential to a man of the cloth.

Even my fleeting glimpse of headlines blaring the Savoy Hotel murder could not dampen my delight, but I did briefly ponder the possibility that another assassin might be searching for me.

Our time together was all too brief before my ship was due to sail, but I wanted to disappear before further implicating my family in any way. The night before departure I described my strategy.

I would leave the country for at least two years, contacting them by coded messages when possible. For safety's sake I would send all communications to Aunt Cordelia, who would forward them discreetly to the addressee. During my absence, I asked that the family submit a formal request to the Federal authorities that my supposed body be transferred to the family plot in Baltimore. This would force the government to produce Robey's corpse (or whoever else they would substitute), and the family would identify it as me. The event should be well publicized in the newspapers, and the authorities would be forced to abandon any further pursuit of John Wilkes Booth, clandestine or otherwise. I would then return from my foreign travels and live incognito somewhere in the West.

My brother readily agreed, and the two of us eventually persuaded Mother that this was the only safe way I could see the family again.

My farewell to Mother was so heart-wrenching that even after so many years I cannot write of it without drenching these pages with my tears. I vowed to see them again somewhere, somehow, and dashed from their room.

I could not sleep. My cabin was small and seemed stifling. Even the brandy was unpalatable, and I decided to walk the deck until we sailed at dawn.

Just as I cracked the door, Joseph shoved his way into the room with uncharacteristic rudeness and poked my chest with his finger. "Sit down, Wilkes," he commanded. "I must speak before you leave."

Before I could ask the question, my brother silenced me

with a dismissive wave of his hand. "Mother knows nothing of this."

The skin of his face was drawn tight and a feral light gleamed from his eyes. He spoke in a voice I had never heard before. "You, Edwin, and even Father have always considered yourselves as such great actors. I detest all you poseurs. But this past week, for Mother's sake, I portrayed a rôle more magnificently than any of you could ever hope to accomplish. For days I've pretended to like, admire, yes, love you, Wilkes. When, as God is my witness, I detest you with every fiber of my being, you murdering pompous ass. Sit, Wilkes," he hissed as I attempted to rise, "or I will send you to the hell you so richly deserve. Sit and listen."

He moved so close I could smell the perfume from his clothes.

"You have disgraced our family name, caused our mother unspeakable grief, and assassinated the greatest man who ever lived. Then you have the unmitigated gall to ask Mother and me to utter monstrous lies to save your worthless neck."

Joseph leaned forward so close his face nearly touched mine.

"And I will do it, dear Brother. But only because my contempt for you and all you represent is outweighed by my love for our sainted mother." He opened the door to leave, then turned back to me with a scowling smile that still tortures my dreams. "As you well know, Wilkes, our drunken father never married Mother until shortly before his death. So all of us, their children, are bastards. The others and I are bastards by accident of birth, but you, you are one because of what you have become. I never want to lay eyes on you again, Brother, in this world or the next. If you return to this country before we lie for you and claim the body, I will put you in a grave myself."

Then he was gone. I slumped to my bed, shaken by Joseph's uncharacteristic fury. Then I shrugged, donned my nightclothes, and slept well.

Before dawn we weighed anchor, the sails were unfurled, and my long journey began on the ebbing tide.

As the sun rose over our stern, I watched San Francisco Bay fade slowly behind me, sighed, and turned to face west for whatever the future might bring.

I would not permit my brother's tirade to wound me as he had intended. After all, Joseph was the black sheep in our family of illustrious thespians. He had become a doctor.

BOOK THREE

For the goodman is not at home,
he is gone a long journey.

Proverbs 7:19

CHAPTER NINE

In the later years of my life, I often amused myself reading newspaper interviews with various people who claimed to have encountered me at wildly improbable sites around the globe. Several such stories reported sightings in locations I not only had never visited in my travels but had never heard of. In such accounts, I was almost invariably described as I appeared on stage posters of the mid-1860s—"long, raven locks, drooping mustache, arched eyebrow, *et cetera.*" Always mention was made of my "characteristic limp".

Until I returned to the United States, my hair was cropped short, and I was clean shaven. My injured leg had healed better than expected, and I took great pride in training myself to walk in a completely normal fashion. How could anyone consider me, a fugitive and esteemed actor, so stupid as to retain my former appearance?

Nevertheless, such fables abounded, consuming reams of newsprint and accounting for increased sales of newspapers, no doubt the sole reason for publication of such banal drivel.

I will render truthfully to the best of my recollection an account of my wanderings in the late 1860s, an adventure more distinguished by the characters I chanced upon rather than my geographical meanderings. Much of this globe-trotting, whether by long sea cruises or uncomfortable treks by land, was tedious to experience and would be boring beyond measure to relate. I passed much of the time alone, voraciously reading newspapers, magazines, and books of every genre. Most novels, especially vapid sagas of romance, I tossed aside in disgust, for my own life and loves were far more interesting than these inane fables.

I became fascinated with the subject of steam propulsion and devoted many hours to poring over technical manuals and nosing about the engine rooms of my ships. Sailing vessels were becoming archaic while steam locomotives and the explosion of railroad construction would soon supplant horse-powered transport on land.

On my previous sea voyages the hybrid vessels on which I traveled were powered by sail when the wind was fair, then paddle wheels to port and starboard to move us when becalmed. Under taut sails we would glide forward smoothly, leaving behind a foaming wake as straight as an arrow, our only sounds the musical creaking of the rigging and the hiss of the water. But when steam power was necessary, our ship became a belching, roaring, soot-laden hell with a track across the water resembling a demented serpent. As swells rocked the keel, one paddle wheel, then the other, would be lifted from the water, and the vessel would veer from side to side despite the best efforts of the helmsman. *Mal de mer* was almost universal among the passengers, and even I could not remain in my cabin under such circumstances.

A blessed relief from such torture was the stability of *Ajax*, our screw propeller-driven vessel, which followed our compass course to the Sandwich Islands precisely, untroubled by wind or wave. Although our cabins were small and functional, the dining hall was commodious, the bar was well stocked, and my fellow passengers, for the most part, were convivial.

One notable exception was an arrogant boor, known only as The Admiral, an appellation no doubt self-bestowed. For hours he would pontificate on any subject, overwhelming his conversational victims with verbosity, and tolerated no interruptions or disagreement.

On this voyage I had chosen the alias of Mark Williams—for no good reason, the name just popped into my brain. The Admiral seemed to select me as his foil for his most bombastic dissertations, unfailingly poking me in the chest to make his point and constantly referring to me simply as Williams.

Not wishing to cause any undue attention to myself, for over a week I tolerated this curmudgeon's verbal inaccuracies with little comment. But one evening after a few brandies I could contain myself no longer. The Admiral had described at length his twisted and inaccurate version of an unsavory incident that had occurred just prior to the recent war. I rose, interrupted him politely, and then quietly tore his account to shreds with irrefutable facts and logic. A smattering of applause and laughter from my fellow passengers at the close of my remarks drove The Admiral from our assembly, his story and ego punctured beyond repair.

In retrospect, I owe my antagonist a great debt, for it was from this episode that I became acquainted with a gentleman soon to become the most acclaimed raconteur of his or any other era.

Sam Clemens was scarcely a few years older than I, but already possessed an inexhaustible potpourri of stories which he related with the humor and eloquence soon to bring him fame and fortune. His remarks were punctuated with tugs on his drooping walrus moustache and stabs with his ever-present pungent cigar. We became great friends before the voyage was over, sharing an affinity for good whiskey and good jokes. However, I declined his invitation to become "wealthy beyond your wildest dreams" by joining him in a venture to develop the burgeoning sugar and cattle industries in the Sandwich Islands.

"Why should we let the missionaries make all the money there?" He smiled. "What in the world would missionaries spend it on?"

I never met a man who possessed more stories or more harebrained schemes doomed to lose money. Ultimately he became renowned for both.

Already he had published some of his tales while working for a newspaper in Nevada Territory and hoped to finance his trip to the islands with narratives of his experiences while there. Certainly he would find it necessary to edit from his accounts most of his and my exploits in this tropical paradise if he held any hope they would be accepted for publication. We devoted a great deal of thought and considerable effort to rescuing the innocent female inhabitants of these blessed islands from the perfidious teachings of pious missionaries.

As Sam once said: "What, sir, would the people of this world be without women? They would be scarce, sir, almighty scarce."

The months spent in these jeweled isles with Sam, surrounded by beautiful women in various stages of undress undulating provocatively, were probably the most agreeable of my life, especially after what all had gone before. But some perverse aspect of my being always seemed to call me to newer adventures even when I was rapturously happy with my present surroundings. Travel to neighboring islands, each with its own unique attractions, failed to entrance my jaded eyes although the panoramas of pristine waterfalls, crashing breakers, and belching volcanoes were forever etched in my memory.

Sam was undoubtedly correct in his assumption that in

these resplendent Sandwich Islands the two of us had glimpsed about all of heaven either of us could ever hope to see and raised enough hell to last for eternity. We also agreed that, if given the choice, it would be difficult to make up our minds which place to go after death. As Sam opined: "Both have their advantages . . . heaven for climate, hell for company."

Sam and I hoisted more than a few brimming glasses to toast our friendship, promises of a reunion, various dignitaries, women we had known, good times, and sundry other topics too numerous to mention. We mumbled a maudlin farewell, and I mounted the gangplank of my steamer with an unsteady gait. Neither of us suspected that the passage of time would render Sam famous beyond his wildest imaginings while my notoriety was rapidly diminishing, and I was fading into obscurity.

I had booked passage for Manila, knowing we would require several stops for fuel, especially if fair winds did not prevail. The voyage would be a long one, and I had the foresight to provide myself with a trunk full of reading material. But I intended to avoid the *ennui* of traversing the vast Pacific with my newest and favorite divertissement, pistol shooting.

Since childhood I had been regarded as a superb marksman but had confined my interest to rifles and shotguns. Early in our friendship Sam had expressed his surprise and disappointment upon learning I had ventured through the untamed American West without owning a handgun.

"The safety of your own skin does not concern me so much as your making a liar out of us who pen tales of the West and its inhabitants. Haven't you read the penny dreadfuls? All men there are handsome and well armed, all women beautiful and virtuous, and all Indians bloodthirsty savages." He puffed mightily on his huge stogie. "Not carrying a gun. Why, sir, such behavior could effect a *coup d'état* of contemporary American literature."

Therefore, to mollify Sam Clemens rather than any abiding interest in handguns, while in Honolulu I purchased a fine brass-framed .32-caliber Prescott revolver, which fit my hand like a glove. Its balance was perfect, rather like an extension of my own arm. In an unbelievably short time I had mastered the technique of accurate instinct shooting. One looks directly at the target rather than aiming, and with practice the pistol hand unerringly points correctly.

Aboard ship I obtained the captain's permission to continue my diversion, using blocks of wood tossed by a crewman into the wake or into the air as targets. When anchored in a harbor, I significantly depleted the population of annoying shore birds and squawking gulls, more difficult but infinitely more satisfying targets.

My marksmanship was soon the talk of our crew, and I never lacked volunteers to fling my targets. Considerable wagering was based on my accuracy, but the lads quickly learned not to bet against me, but only among themselves. Needless to say, for the entire voyage my skills earned for me the utmost respect and deference by the sailors, who attended my every need.

Their services were not altogether altruistic, for they and I won considerable sums from personnel at our fueling stops in isolated atolls. These lonely souls were starved for any entertainment, however costly. As a matter of fact, I paid for the entire voyage with my revolver, and my purse was much fatter on arrival in Manila than when I had left Honolulu.

By that time I had also perfected a lightning-fast extraction of my weapon from either shoulder or hip holster. My friend, Sam Clemens, could be very proud of me now, and any future adversary rash enough to test my expertise would enter hell long before I.

We entered the confines of magnificent Manila Bay with the wind at our backs, facing a sunset of such staggering beauty I was riveted with wonder. Later I was told that such vivid panoramas resulted from volcanic particles suspended in the atmosphere, but even the beauty of the Sandwich Islands did not compare with these vistas. No landscape before or since could compare with my first view of this sumptuous harbor.

We glided by a tadpole-shaped island on our left, crossed the bay, and anchored by lamplight. My belongings and I were transported to the hotel by *calesa,* an ornately decorated two-wheeled horse cart. The rutted muddy streets of the capital were flanked by magnificent Spanish cathedrals towering above squalid thatched Filipino nipa huts.

The Filipinos I met were unfailingly courteous and friendly, exceedingly proud of their homeland and gracious hosts. Although Spain had ruled these islands for centuries, after only a few days I could sense an almost palpable loathing of the Filipinos for their conquerors and the contempt of Spanish officials for their subjects.

Even this uncomfortable malaise could not mask the beauty of my surroundings, and I resolved to tarry a few months here and tour a land as foreign to me as the moon.

I first ventured to the mountainous terrain of upper Luzon and relaxed for several days in the delightfully cool village of Baguio. I had hoped to travel farther north to visit the legendary artisans and spectacular rice terraces of that region. However, my interest waned after I was informed that Igorot tribesmen of that area were avid head-hunters, particularly interested in obtaining the pallid craniums of missionaries. Even my Filipino guides would not venture there during Igorot "hunting season". Heads were prized during that time in some sort of mating ritual, serving, I suppose, as dowries. I certainly had no desire to lose my head to these benighted tribesmen but was much more apprehensive of somehow being mistaken for a missionary.

From Baguio we followed a serpentine trail down the mountains to the tiny bayside village of San Fernando and sailed in an enormous outrigger canoe down the east coast of Luzon to Manila.

En route from the quay to my hotel, I halted the *calesa* to investigate a murmuring assemblage of Filipinos just in front of the old Spanish fort near the heart of Manila. In halting English my driver explained that a man accused of insulting a Spanish officer was to be executed—beheaded. Surely this could not be true in these modern times. Hanging, death by firing squad perhaps, but certainly not beheading.

Curiosity overcame my better judgment, and I slowly elbowed my way through the milling, grumbling crowd to a clear area ringed by uniformed Spanish soldiers armed with bayoneted rifles. In the center posed an imperious Spanish officer who droned haltingly from an official-looking document, which he held at arm's length. I understood not a word he said, and from the expressions of faces in the crowd the spectators were as ignorant of the proclamation's content as I. Two soldiers stood opposite the officer clutching between them a blindfolded Filipino in peasant garb, his hands bound securely behind his back. They faced a blighted wooden stump which obviously had been used for such occasions many times before. A swarthy priest garbed in exceedingly shabby and soiled vestments stood just to one side. From his bearing, it was obvious he was there to provide his church's sanction to the proceedings, rather than to proffer any commiseration to the prisoner.

The officer finished his tirade and unsheathed his saber. He spoke curtly to the soldiers. They quickly shoved the hapless victim to the stump and forced him to his knees. As the Spaniard raised his sword, the victim defiantly cried out an unintelligible phrase. I recognized only the word *Dios*.

The officer flashed downward with his saber but, incompetent to the last, failed to completely cleave the man's neck. Blood gushed from the peasant's severed arteries, drenching the priest who turned away and dropped to his knees, retching. The victim's legs quivered, and his sphincters relaxed as his body rolled from the stump. A foul odor of warm blood and feces spread like a cloud over the horrified moaning spectators. Women, and many men, swooned.

The officer screamed at the two ghastly pale soldiers, and they obediently dragged the dying man back into position. The blindfold had become dislodged, and I could see his eyes blink and the tetanic grimaces of his face. The saber descended again, and it was over except for the keening of the crowd.

I turned and forced my way back to the street; all the beauty of these islands erased by this one mad act.

History may never deal with me kindly, but no one could ever suggest I was an incompetent executioner.

I was eager to leave Manila and hoped to book passage for a direct uninterrupted journey possibly to India and beyond, but no large ships would be available for months. Therefore I found myself traveling on a grimy little packet hauling odiferous cattle and natives through the southern islands to Zamboanga. We would exchange our cargo in this port for a load of mahogany lumber bound for Java. This route would take us dangerously close to Jolo and Basilan Islands, homeland of barbarous Muslim pirates, merciless predators of the Sulu and Celebes Seas.

Forewarned is forearmed, so I increased my armament with the purchase of two Colt .44 revolvers. They were not as fancy or as easy to handle as my Prescott, but they were reliable weapons and ammunition was readily available. If only Sam Clemens could see me now.

The pungent journey to Zamboanga was without incident, although I longed for some camphor to inhale as temporary relief from the stench. A barely acceptable substitute was the aroma of reasonably decent rum, and I medicated myself liberally throughout the trip.

I found Zamboanga to be a rather charming small city with more native than Spanish influence in its people and architecture. However, I spent more time expending ammunition in my daily practice with my weapons than seeing the sights.

Our ship sat low in the water, slowed by its heavy cargo of lumber, and its deep keel mandated that we stay in the channels to avoid disastrous encounters with a maze of coral reefs.

The only other passengers were a Dutchman, his wife, and two young daughters returning to their plantation near Batavia on the island of Java. None of them spoke a word of English, and we communicated briefly at meals by smiles and gestures. I was not even sure I understood their last name—"Chilled Beets"—or so it sounded to me.

At dawn on the third day, I was awakened by a loud racket from the foredeck and peered out to spy two red-sailed vessels heading directly for us. I dressed hastily and joined the Chinese captain.

As best I could understand his panicky jabber, these were indeed pirates heading for us. The channel was too narrow to turn about, and the villains sailed much faster than this old scow could manage with its cargo. I rushed to my cabin and loaded the pistols, then pantomimed to the Dutchman that he should lock himself and his family in their cabin. He did not need any persuading.

I returned to the captain and with significant effort convinced him to continue steering and keep us off of the reefs. I surmised he had already assumed his situation was hopeless, and we would be massacred. Our remaining crew members were cowering in the engine room awaiting their fate. I crouched out of sight behind a starboard bulkhead and waited.

The two dhows approached rapidly. A squat, barrel-chested Oriental in the bow of the closest boat screamed at our terrified captain, who slowed our ship almost to a stop. The pirates brandished their machetes and swords while they shouted what I presumed to be vile threats. With practiced efficiency the cut-throats made fast their vessels to ours and proceeded to board. Each boat contained six men.

Excellent, I would not have to reload.

I stepped from behind the bulkhead and fired six times. I laid the smoking hot weapon on the deck, then switched the other loaded Colt from my left hand to my right and calmly fired six times more. I carefully set this pistol down and cut the two boats loose to drift away with their grisly cargo of twelve dead men.

The whole experience was much more pleasurable than shooting sea birds and afforded equally good target practice.

CHAPTER TEN

Our progress through Makassar Strait into the Sea of Java was unimpeded by any additional untoward events, and was, for me, rather boring. I amused myself by pacing the deck for exercise, reading, and of course my continued interest in the functions and intermarriage of steam and sail for propelling our vessel.

Concerned with conserving ammunition should we encounter another band of aquatic pillagers, I limited my target practice to only one or two days a week, much to the dismay of the Dutchman's daughters. These young ladies seemed entranced by my demonstrations, giggling and applauding at my successes, moaning piteously like two kittens on occasion of my rare misses. I enjoyed their company for a time, but even adulation can become tedious, and I found myself spending more and more time in my quarters entertaining myself with a good book.

The plump Dutchman and his rotund, pink-cheeked omnivorous wife almost smothered me with gratitude after the pirate episode, but soon returned to their ultimate passion—consuming everything on board except the rigging.

After my initial repugnance at their table manners, or lack thereof, I became fascinated with the truly marvelous efficiency with which this couple stoked the raging fires of their digestive systems. A distant glazed stare entered their eyes as soon as they were comfortably seated in their overly stressed rattan chairs, and the contest would begin. With a spoon in either hand the contents of each platter were ladled expertly into their mouths without a molecule of spillage and seemed to disappear without mastication. Empty trenchers were adroitly replaced by a perspiring steward, careful to keep his hands safe from the dangerous maws. Finale to each performance was signaled by tandem belches of a magnitude to stimulate the mating instinct of elephants within a radius of several miles.

I once idly wondered how the couple had stopped eating long enough to conceive their attractive daughters, and, considering their prodigious bulk, how such an act could have been accomplished without the use of scaffolding. But the mental image this conveyed caused me to lose my appetite for quite some time and I willed my brain not to recall it.

Upon arrival in Batavia, I had planned immediately to book passage for Europe, presuming that ships should depart from here regularly *en route* to Amsterdam, maybe even London. But the Dutchman insistently conveyed to me his determination that I must first accompany him on an errand of great importance. His massive wife and lovely daughters almost smothered me in hugs and tearful kisses while murmuring unintelligible expressions of gratitude. They climbed into an ornate waiting carriage and waved good bye until they disappeared in the noisy, roiling mob at dockside. A constantly smiling livered servant commanding a brace of magnificent steeds harnessed to a regal coach drove the Dutchman and me into the heart of the city.

We halted in front of a massive columned bank and entered, whereupon the Dutchman was greeted effusively by a multitude of fawning employees. It was obvious that he was the owner or primary officer of the facility, especially when we were seated in his lavishly decorated office. He spoke briefly to one of his staff, who promptly disappeared but soon returned with a sheaf of documents and another employee who spoke heavily accented English.

"Mister Schillebeeck say to tell you his thank you for the saving of himself and family. He say please with him these papers to sign."

Of course I could not understand the details of the transaction, whatever it might be, but certainly did not wish to offend my host, and so penned my signature wherever indicated by the efficient, obsequious clerk. The Dutchman scrawled his name below mine, smiled ingratiatingly, and lit our cigars. He joined me in puffing contentedly, then spoke at some length to the translator, smiled again, and shook my hand.

"Mister Schillebeeck . . . ." The translator looked as if he could not believe what he was saying. "He say if not for you so brave to be, he and family would be die. So, he say now you and he in business be together." The man swallowed audibly and continued. "He now to you give ten percent this bank. You no have work no more long in you life."

Some fortunes are outright gifts while others are earned. Although Mr. Schillebeeck's generosity took me aback for a moment, I could not help but reflect that except for me, neither he nor his family would be alive to reap the rewards of his prosperity. And, after all, his only vice seemed to be gluttony while I could distribute my new-found wealth among any number of hedonistic pursuits.

For the next several months I toured Java from one palm-shaded pristine shore to another, my senses all but overwhelmed by the scented verdure, savage pulsing rhythms of their primitive instruments, and pliant, voluptuous women enticingly bare-breasted. But this Eden was not without its serpents. Among tribes of the mountainous regions, cannibalism was widely practiced, with brain-eating a particularly fulsome delight. Certainly there was no danger this unique custom would gain acceptance in official Washington, for it would require the sacrifice of an inordinate number of politicians to provide enough raw material for even a light snack.

The guides employed by my benefactor apparently had been instructed to accede to my every whim, and I was not permitted to pay for anything. But weeks of such uninterrupted bliss proved to be exhausting, and my old wanderlust began to resurface.

There is certainly no chance that I will ever experience heaven, but I am sure that for me it would be tedious to the extreme. Everlasting life alone suggests insufferable boredom.

I returned to Batavia and, after a sumptuous farewell banquet provided by the Schillebeecks, embarked on a long voyage across the southern Indian Ocean to Capetown and from thence to London. The Suez Canal was nearing completion, and my Dutch hosts had begged me to stay in Java until this much abbreviated route was available, but I would not be dissuaded. Many times while at sea I regretted this stubborn decision. Although my vessel was comfortable enough, and I amused myself with my books and pistols, weeks of gazing at nothing but water to every horizon would dull the senses of a Stoic.

As we wended our way up the west shore of Africa, I obtained little relief from my impatience during our infrequent pauses at odious coastal cities. It continues to mystify me why so many nations vied for portions of this blighted continent. The climate is beastly, the winds and currents are erratic, and the seaside inhabitants I encountered on my brief sojourns in port are for the most part decidedly uninteresting. Eking out a meager existence consumes these benighted citizens' daily lives, and their only recreation is procreation.

At long last, London. Civilization personified. Less than a week after we docked, I had rented a comfortable flat, purchased a new wardrobe, sampled excellent whiskey, and satisfied biological needs too long delayed by arduous sea travel. Then it was time for my return to the theatre, albeit for the present as a member of the audience. Farces, musicals, comedies, dramas, I saw them all. Anything worth doing is worth doing to excess, I say, and this applies particularly to the pursuit of happiness.

Much to my amazement and delight, I discovered that the trans-Atlantic telegraph cable was now operational from London to New York. During my clandestine involvement with Confederate planners in Canada during the recent conflict, we had learned of efforts to lay this cable from England to America through Newfoundland. Considerable discussion ensued about means by which we could thwart this operation, but no action proved necessary. The war had ended before successful telegraphy via cable was accomplished.

I crafted a pre-arranged cryptic message which was transmitted to New York and on to Aunt Cordelia, then from her to Mother. She would at least know I was still alive and keeping her in my thoughts as always.

Another surprise awaited me. While searching through newspaper advertisements for a performance of Shakespeare, I discovered that my traitorous brother Edwin was in London, appearing in *Hamlet*. Two nights later I attended his incursion upon the London stage. While his execution of the rôle was adequate, his interpretation of the character never attained the introspection such a complex classic demanded. The applause was polite, though sparse. I could not resist the opportunity to gloat.

After the theatre closed, I loitered outside in the shadows and waited until a carriage was summoned for Edwin. He bade good night to a thin gathering of effete admirers and entered his coach. Before he could signal his driver, I peered through the window and spoke in my most dulcet tones.

"Father and I were always better Hamlets than you, Edwin. Please confine yourself to the rôle of coward, dear Brother. You do it so well."

I disappeared before he could reply.

To paraphrase Shakespeare: "Let us make medicine of our great revenge, to cure this deadly grief."

The encounter with Edwin afforded me an abiding satisfaction akin to the inner warmth of excellent brandy and provided the perfect finale to my pleasant stay in London. Somehow my sojourn through the American West, although infinitely less enjoyable at the time than Java, London, or the Sandwich Islands, had left me with an almost magnetic attraction to that boundless land.

But chaos still reigned in the land of my birth. Reconstruction was a bitter pill on which the Southern states still gagged while guerrilla warfare and banditry raged unchecked throughout the Border States. In Washington, President Johnson had fired Secretary Stanton. Long simmering rancor and controversy erupted, which resulted in impeachment proceedings being filed against the President. His removal from office failed by only one vote. Testimony presented during his trial refueled speculation about an occult conspiracy to assassinate Lincoln, but such material was largely concealed from the public.

In December, 1868, President Johnson pardoned all

those involved in the Civil War, and the outcry over an assassination conspiracy died to a faint murmur. It seemed Z had cleverly defused all attempts to expose him and his cohorts.

In 1867, Mother had filed a brief requesting "my body" be returned to the Booth family for Christian burial. Two years later, her request was still pending. I would keep my word, therefore, and not return to them until the matter was settled. England disappeared astern as our ship headed southwest for Mexico, and, after a tranquil, uneventful voyage, we docked at Vera Cruz.

CHAPTER ELEVEN

Unknowingly I had leaped into a roiling cauldron of war, intrigue, and perfidy. The French Emperor Maximilian had been defeated by Mexican forces in the summer of 1867 and he was summarily executed by a firing squad. Benito Juárez was elected president by a wide margin, but faced serious problems from the day of his inauguration.

Two devastating wars in recent history had left the Mexican treasury almost empty. Maximilian's fate had fostered deep resentment among the European powers, resulting in dried-up markets and shrunken investment capital. To raise money, President Juárez sold off lands expropriated from the Catholic Church to the highest bidders, predominantly big landowners who had supported his liberal cause. Peasant farmers, expecting a just share in the distribution of land, felt betrayed. Joining former soldiers who had fought against Juárez and Indians who had also been dispossessed, bands of farmers staged innumerable uprisings throughout the country or were driven into outright banditry.

In 1868, two massive peasant revolts were eventually suppressed by federal troops after a difficult and bloody campaign characterized by revolting atrocities.

But the Indian problem continued. Mayan tribes effectively controlled southeastern Mexico, and Apaches dominated the north. As settlers and U.S. cavalry moved into the American Southwest, Apache incursions, led by Cochise and his successors, exploded into the sparsely populated and less well-protected regions south of the Río Grande.

Over 15,000 inhabitants of this area were massacred.

Juárez had been often described as the "Mexican Abraham Lincoln", and Lincoln had been a strong supporter of Juárez as early as 1857. In the midst of his war against the Confederacy, Lincoln lavished arms and munitions on Juárez. The favor was returned when a delegation from the Confederate government was sent to request aid from Mexico. John Pickett, leader of the delegation, was thrown into a Mexican jail, then expelled from the country on order from President Juárez.

Political machinations, particularly those in foreign countries, interested me about as much as acquiring a heat rash, but my sympathies would certainly lie with those who opposed a "Mexican Lincoln".

As I prepared to disembark at Vera Cruz, I learned that my ship would leave in a few days to travel up the coast to Tampico, and from that port on to Galveston, Texas. My same cabin was available, and I had no urgent desire to join the primitive ox-cart caravan over the mountains to Mexico City. Therefore I remained on board until we sailed, except for frequent imperative excursions into the city to sample the local culture, particularly the mores of selected comely *señoritas*. As I arrived not speaking a word of Spanish, the challenge was rendered even more delightful.

Although not possessing the total lack of modesty and sexual aggressiveness of the Pacific Islanders, I found the Mexican women to be coyly flirtatious with an intriguing shyness on initial contact often followed by a feral abandon infrequently encountered and invariably appreciated. A decided and welcome contrast to English women I had known, who generally approached such activities with the haughty disdain usually reserved for their dealings with servants, and the horizontal enthusiasm of corpses.

112

Luck or fate continued to bless me, for I learned soon after arrival in Tampico that the caravan from Vera Cruz had been ambushed by *banditos* and slaughtered to a man.

One often determines his own luck, and I trust no one on this earth except Mother and myself. So before leaving Tampico, I secured an ample supply of ammunition for my Colts, and as much as I could find for my Prescott. These weapons would most assuredly be effectively lethal in my hands at close range, but oft-times a battle is won by artillery rather than close combat. Therefore, I substantially brightened the day of an obliging gunsmith with the purchase of a .44-caliber, 16-shot brass Henry rifle, and cartridge-filled bandoleers. For the *coup de grâce* I acquired a 10-gauge Parker double-barreled shotgun.

Next I commissioned a fine-tooled saddle to be adapted with bags and scabbards to accommodate the new weaponry and began my search for a proper mount. Almost an entire day was consumed with this selection for, although price was immaterial, I required a fleet steed that could manage the additional weight of my arsenal.

A coal-black, part-Arabian gelding with the peculiar name of Corazón fit my needs precisely, and I was soon ready to travel. The unrelenting Mexican sun was beastly, but I could not abide the huge, uncomfortable sombreros and shaded myself with a stout British umbrella. This appendage was a constant source of poorly concealed amusement for the Mexicans, and I am sure their incomprehensible comments were far from flattering. But it was just as well that their remarks were meaningless to me, or I would have been forced to kill some of them to improve the manners of any survivors.

Only a few tedious days into our journey as we were entering the foothills of the mountains, I learned that one of the armed outriders in our caravan spoke rudimentary English. This young man had been employed for a time by a Scotsman in Tampico, so even his English was difficult to comprehend. But we learned each other's language together, and our efforts masked the discomforts of our plodding pace over the serpentine trail. Federico—Rico—was an apt pupil and patient teacher. By the time we reached San Luis Potosi, we were speaking to each other in halting, frequently hilarious sentences and communicating well.

Ignoring Rico's protestations, I bought a fine Colt revolver for him to replace the rusted relic he carried, and a nice horse instead of the ancient nag he had been riding. We pleasured ourselves in the *cantinas* for a few days while the freight was assembled and loaded, then left for Zacatecas.

During our stay in Potosi, Rico had told me he had heard of "some *gringos* from the war" who lived with their families in Mexico, but he did not know exactly where, possibly south near Guadalajara. No doubt these were remnants of Confederate forces that had not surrendered, escaped across the Río Grande from Texas, and been joined by their families. I ached to see someone from "home" but could never reveal my true identity to them for obvious reasons.

Zacatecas was the terminal depot for our freighters. They unloaded, drank themselves blind for a couple of days, then made preparations for their return with a new load back to Tampico. I persuaded Rico to go on with me, at least as far as Durango, so we could continue our lessons and, to tell the truth, our friendship. He was the only person whose company I truly had enjoyed since Sam Clemens.

Rico and I experienced no difficulty in obtaining employment as guards for mining supplies and equipment being shipped to Durango for distribution.

Language lessons and occasional target practice passed the time for Rico and me as the days ground by. I had noticed that comments about the umbrella had almost entirely disappeared after an initial demonstration of my weaponry. Or had the freighters been warned by Rico that I now could understand much of their conversation?

A couple of days out of Durango, Rico rode out far ahead to scout for rock slides, and I endured an unusually long day riding silently without his cheerful company. As the merciless sun waned in the late afternoon, I became increasingly uneasy. A lone rider in this mountainous region was a tempting target. I loosened my pistols in their holsters and trotted out well ahead of the wagon train.

The buzzards had found him first. These hideous scavengers reluctantly abandoned the feast as I approached and labored to lift their swollen bodies to a nearby perch. They waited patiently.

Rico was hacked almost beyond recognition, limbs virtually dismembered. His genitals had been torn away and stuffed deeply into his throat. The murderous bastards had also killed his horse, slashing its throat and disemboweling the poor beast. The sickening smell of blood, offal, and waste was unbearable. For a moment horror obliterated my reflexes, then I screamed vile oaths of anger and frustration while macabre echoes resonated down the cañon.

Exerting the superhuman effort necessary to control my emotions, I commenced a cool, calculating exercise in mental dexterity to analyze quickly the situation and generate a solution.

Rico had been killed at close range, probably with ma-

chetes. There were no bullet wounds. Therefore, his at-
tackers were able to approach him without rousing his
suspicions and probably had no firearms of their own. Indians, especially Apaches, were known for mutilating the
bodies of their victims, so Rico had told me. But most of
the Indian tribes were well armed with stolen rifles and
would probably have shot him from ambush. Apaches usually had little use for pistols except to barter for rifles, and
Rico's weapon seemed to be missing.

When I moved my friend's body to search for his revolver, I found the crude note pinned to the flesh of his
bloodied chest with a cactus thorn. My Spanish was barely
adequate to translate the substance of the message as:
**Leave burros and supplies here or die. We are
watching**.

I scanned the sheer walls and brim of the cañon towering
above me. Not a leaf stirred, but I experienced the uneasy
sensation that my every move was being intently observed.

Rico's killers must be poorly armed peasant *banditos*
hoping to capture our wagon train of supplies, especially
the weapons and explosives, but lacking sufficient rifles for
an effective ambush. However, they knew this terrain intimately, and if necessary could slowly pick us off, one by
one. As the heavily laden burros and their handlers approached, I concocted my plan.

I covered Rico's torn body as best I could with my coat
and halted the caravan. In broken Spanish and gestures, I
advised the men of our situation and assured them they
would survive only if they followed my instructions precisely. After peering fearfully about them, the drovers
bunched the wagons together and tied the pack-laden
burros closely to them as I had instructed. Each of eight
burros carried four cases of dynamite, and one wagon held

ten cases, in addition to drill steel, shovels, picks, and several barrels of nails. I had no experience in the use of explosives, but assumed the detonation of these materials should produce the desired effect.

Very, very cautiously I distributed blasting caps among the cases and tied a large bouquet of caps to the outside of the crates in the wagon containing the explosives.

At my signal the men scattered in different directions like startled quail and disappeared. I leaped aboard Corazón and galloped over the next hill out of sight, then slid to a stop, dismounted, and tied my panting mount to a gnarled stubby tree. With my pistols in their holsters and a bandoleer of ammunition, I slipped the Henry from its scabbard and returned the way I had come.

From my concealed vantage point behind a mound of boulders slightly less than 100 yards away, I surveyed the scene. Nothing stirred except the twitching ears and switching tails of the mules and burros as pesky insects plagued them. I fixed the sights of my Henry on the cluster of blasting caps and waited. For several interminable minutes nothing happened. Swarms of insects had found me and buzzed annoyingly around my head, but I dared not move.

I blinked the sweat from my eyes. When they cleared, a man was standing precisely where I had been looking a moment before. One after another men appeared from the bleak landscape as if they were animated mushrooms sprouting before my astonished gaze. Eventually a dozen or more ragged figures shuffled toward the road, each carrying a large knife or wicked-looking machete. The first man to rise, obviously their leader, also carried Rico's pistol.

When all the *banditos* were fervidly swarming over the wagons and animals, I fired the Henry.

Even I had not imagined such carnage. The explosion's blast took my breath away. Pieces of wagon, body parts of men and animals, drill steel, broken picks, shovels, and dead buzzards rained down for an eternity. A fine red mist permeated the atmosphere and had not disappeared long after the dissonant, ear-splitting echoes had died away.

I stumbled down the hill, my ears still ringing, and dispatched a burro and two men, or what remained of them, with my pistols. Nothing else moved. Even the air was still, and all the insects were gone. Fragments of wagon, bloody pieces of burro, and barely recognizable human body parts were splattered in vivid colors against the near cañon wall like some obscene mural. A huge crater more than adequate to serve as Rico's grave had been blasted in the roadbed, and I gently lowered my friend into the cavity. I had found his battered pistol by the roadside and lay it on his chest before filling the hole with stones. The rest of the scene I left to be cleaned by the eager buzzards, already circling overhead.

Without a backward glance or twinge of regret, I began walking back to retrieve Corazón and continue my trek to Durango. On the crest of a distant peak I spotted a figure, presumably one of the wagoneers, who waved his sombrero in a gesture of farewell, then disappeared over the horizon. This man may well have been the original author of a legend, much embellished over the years and recited in Mexico to this day, which tells of *El Pistolero y su Sombria*— The Gunman with his Umbrella—who single-handedly vanquished an entire rebel army.

Ever vigilant, umbrella held high, I traveled alone to Durango without an untoward incident. In that city I tarried only long enough to replace my wardrobe and personal items, which unfortunately had been stored in one of the wagons with the dynamite.

Unwilling to burden Corazón with the additional load and not wanting to be accused by disgruntled mine owners for the loss of an entire shipment of essential supplies, I decided to leave immediately by stagecoach for Chihuahua City. Corazón would be tethered behind, and I would break the monotony of the trip by riding him from time to time. This decision may well have saved my life and certainly saved the lives of innumerable Apaches.

We had traveled without incident to only a day's journey south of our destination, but I could endure the constant jouncing of our stagecoach and the incomprehensible chatter of my fellow passengers no longer. My tired eyes were glazed with boredom and discomfort when I spied a spectacular alabaster *hacienda* in the hills some miles to the west of us. Corazón was in need of exercise, and I certainly needed an interruption in the tedium, so I mounted up and left the stage to proceed onward toward Durango. I would rejoin them after my brief respite.

Corazón seemed to enjoy the gallop as much as I did after nearly a week of patiently trotting in the choking dust behind the coach. We reached the ranch house in minutes.

The place was deserted and deathly still. I shoved open a sagging gate and beheld a vista of utter devastation. Everything flammable in the compound was charred or burned to ashes. A myriad of rustic crosses marked graves placed haphazardly throughout the courtyard, some littered with desiccated flowers scattered by the winds. Shafts of arrows and bullet marks marred the crumbling walls. The Apaches must have raided here long ago. Apparently there were no survivors of the massacre, and no one had dared to return.

I wandered around the compound for several hours but found little of interest and the desecration of this once-lovely site became increasingly depressing.

I returned to the road at a leisurely canter and was contemplating target practice on the lizards and creatures scurrying about but realized gunshots might attract unwelcome attention. This prescient conclusion proved valid as I topped a small rise to encounter another appalling scene.

The stagecoach was in ruins, toppled on its side. Baggage and loose clothing was scattered across the desert floor, flapping crazily in the gusty dry wind. The bodies of eviscerated mules lay in their traces. Naked corpses of the driver and passengers, mutilated beyond recognition, were crumpled like bloody dolls around the coach. As I dismounted, I heard a faint moan from one of the Mexicans who, unbelievably, was still alive. Only his lidless eyes moved in a silent plea for mercy. The sound of a gunshot might attract their assailants, so I extracted an abandoned lance from one of the corpses and thrust it through the wretched man's heart.

Discretion is always the better part of valor. I mounted Corazón without further delay and galloped unmolested to Chihuahua. There was nothing else I could have done. Besides, I now had need to purchase yet another wardrobe.

CHAPTER TWELVE

From Chihuahua the main trail extended almost directly north to the Texas border at El Paso del Norte and on to Santa Fé. A shorter, less-traveled route led northwest to cross the Río Grande at Ojinaga. I chose the latter, hoping to lessen my chances of additional encounters with Apaches or *banditos*. However, as a man of my word, I would not enter the States until I had contacted Mother and learned that "my body" had been safely buried in the family plot, and the hunt for me was over.

I had taken a room in a fairly respectable hotel with an intermittently edible cuisine and again purchased clothing and essentials. Telegraphic communications had reached Chihuahua, so I was able to dispatch a coded message to dear Aunt Cordelia, and she would forward it to Mother. The telegrapher advised me that several days to a week or more would elapse before I could expect a reply, so I commenced a diligent perusal of the city's watering holes and palaces of pleasure.

One evening at the Cantina de Nogalito, I joined an on-going poker game with some drovers from Santa Fé solely out of boredom and the desire for conversation in English rather than my halting Spanish. Two other participants were small-time cattle buyers from the Texas Big Bend country visiting Mexico to negotiate the purchase of a rangy longhorn bull or two for breeding stock. From their speech and manners I suspected they were more accustomed to stealing bulls than buying them.

While I was steadily relieving these Texans of their excess *dinero*, one of the spectators caught my attention. From his swarthy complexion and clothing I would have taken the young man for an Indian, probably Apache. But his shoulder-length greasy hair was definitely red, held in place by a rawhide thong which supported a patch over his left eye. The right was a startling blue—the eye of a killer. I inclined my head toward the apparition and asked one of my Mexican companions at the table: *"¿Quién es el hombre con ojo uno?"*

"I speak English," the stripling grumbled, "and Mexican, and Apache. Who the hell are you?"

This was my introduction to Mickey Free, unwilling pawn in the infamous Bascom affair. This episode had occurred nearly ten years past and had resulted in the loss of almost 5,000 lives and the destruction of hundreds of thousands of dollars' worth of property in northern Mexico, Arizona, and New Mexico. Accounts of the débacle involving Lieutenant Bascom, the Apache leader, Cochise, the young boy, Mickey Free, and the consequences of this disaster had even garnered headlines in Eastern newspapers during the war years.

Early in 1861, a rogue band of Coyotero Apaches raided the pitiful ranch in southeastern Arizona territory owned by a thoroughly unsavory character named John Ward. Along with twenty head of cattle, the Apaches relieved Ward of Mickey, the twelve-year-old, one-eyed son of his Mexican mistress.

Ward reported the raid to the commander of nearby Fort Buchanan, but blamed the raid on the Chiricahua Apaches, specifically a band led by their famous chief, Cochise. Next morning, George Bascom, a green lieutenant with little or no knowledge of Apaches, was placed in command of a detachment of troops with orders to "pursue and chastise the marauding Indians."

Cochise and his followers, unaware of the raid at Ward's ranch or the approaching soldiers, were wintering in the mountains near Apache Pass, a way station on the Butterfield stage road.

Bascom sent a messenger to Cochise requesting a parley, and Cochise, suspecting nothing, brought his wife, two of his children, and three warriors to the encampment.

In Bascom's tent Cochise denied any knowledge of the raid and even offered his services to negotiate with the Apaches holding the boy. But Bascom had surrounded the tent with his troopers and told Cochise that he would hold him and his family hostage until Mickey was released.

Cochise drew a knife, slashed his way through the canvas tent, and escaped. But his family was held prisoner. Early the next morning Cochise demanded the release of his wife and children while Lieutenant Bascom, still not convinced of Cochise's innocence, stubbornly insisted that Cochise release Mickey Free. Gunfire ended the negotiations.

From the crest of a nearby hill the following morning, Cochise exhibited a bound stagecoach driver he had captured and offered the hapless man to Bascom in exchange for the safe return of his family. Bascom again refused, reiterating his demand for the release of young Mickey.

The next day Cochise captured a wagon train, killed nine Mexican drovers, captured three Americans, and burned the wagons. He sent a note to Bascom, written by the stagecoach driver, requesting an exchange of prisoners, but Bascom still refused. Cochise then tortured and killed the drovers and the American captives, returned to his mountain redoubt, and vowed further revenge.

When Bascom and his troopers discovered the bodies, he

buried them under four oak trees, released Cochise's wife and children to find their own way home across the desert, and summarily hanged all six Apache prisoners to dangle over the new graves.

The Bascom episode transformed Cochise and his followers from peaceful Indians, co-operative with the government, to the scourge of the southwestern United States and northern Mexico.

Federal troops had largely abandoned their forts in Texas, Arizona, and New Mexico, to join their war against the Confederacy. This departure left settlers and ranchers of these areas defenseless against Indian marauders. The population of Arizona diminished from 34,000 in 1860 to 10,000 in 1870. Cochise remained at large.

Mickey Free grew to adulthood among the Coyotero Apaches, and at the time of our meeting was employed as a scout for freighters on the Chihuahua Trail. These men valued him primarily for his ability to converse in English, Spanish, and Apache, for he was reputed to be *"muy loco en cabeza"* and allegedly possessed the disposition of a peeled rattlesnake.

Admittedly I had become increasingly vexed by the oafish behavior and boorish manners of most Americans I had endured during my travels. Undoubtedly this long-simmering ire explains my permitting a rude remark from this insolent one-eyed whelp to transcend my accustomed implacability.

Without rising, and before the lad had finished his question, the Colt appeared in my outstretched arm scant inches from his good eye.

"Show some respect, you young fool," I rasped, "or I will blast your sole remaining eye out through your obviously empty head."

His childish reply and expression of total amazement were so unexpected I holstered my revolver and dissolved into gales of laughter.

"Goddalmighty, mister, would you show me how to do that trick with your gun?"

It was the inauspicious beginning of a long friendship.

This rough-edged youth had already suffered more hardship and harsh treatment in his slightly more than twenty years of life than most men endure in a lifetime.

His mother had been a Mexican prostitute in Chihuahua and no one, especially his mother, knew or cared who his true father was. In a moment of pique she had named her unwanted infant Mickey Free for a transient customer known only as Mickey, who had treated her abominably, then refused to pay.

John Ward had won Mickey's mother from her madam in a rigged poker game and, despite her pleas, took her and the boy back to his so-called ranch as virtual slaves. Ward abused the boy almost daily and worked him to exhaustion. One particularly severe beating destroyed the youngster's left eye. Many times, as he grew older, Mickey considered running away but was afraid of the reprisals Ward would enact on his mother. Besides, no child could hope to survive in the unforgiving, snake-infested desert that surrounded their miserable dwelling.

Young Mickey was cowed into terrified silence after his abduction by the Coyotero Apaches and expected to be tortured or killed at any moment. Even so, the boy was thankful to escape Ward's evil grasp. Much to his surprise, his captors treated him as a prized possession, initially because of his value in bartering with the whites, but later with genuine affection. The life of the Apache warriors was hard, but the boy's brutal childhood had enabled Mickey to tolerate any adversity. In a few weeks he was an accepted member of the tribe, and shortly thereafter began his tutelage under the guidance of Minocado, grandson of the famous chief, Mangas Coloradas.

For the next eight or so years Mickey traveled, learned, and in essence became an Apache. According to him, these were the happiest days of his life. He accompanied the warriors on forays into Mexico for cattle, horses, and slaves, but was never allowed to participate in attacks on the whites. The Apaches reasoned that, if he deserted them or was captured, the white-eyes would hang him as a murderer.

In 1863, Federal troops captured Mangas Coloradas and tortured the old man by holding white-hot bayonets to his feet. After his death they boiled the flesh from his decapitated head and sent his skull to a museum in Washington. When news of this debased wickedness reached the Coyoteros, Mickey was kept in camp while Apache tribes unleashed attacks of unparalleled ferocity on unfortunate inhabitants of the American Southwest. Broken promises, betrayals, and acts of unspeakable barbarism by all combatants characterized the Indian wars of the 1860s on both sides of the Mexican border. By the early 1870s, the ruthless methods and superior firepower of government forces had suppressed any effective resistance by the Indians, but sporadic raids and uprisings continued to plague the region.

Minocado convinced Mickey to flee across the border into Mexico and avoid forced confinement with the Coyoteros on a reservation. With his language skills and knowledge of the country, the young man experienced no difficulty in obtaining employment with wagon trains plying the Chihuahua Trail.

His Apache tutors had furnished Mickey an unequaled

education in survival skills while our friendship was cemented by my intense curriculum for him in the Wade Prescott School of Pleasurable Pursuits.

I had assumed that pseudonym on arriving in Mexico and had found no valid reason for changing it. Wade, I had chosen from the first name of a Confederate general I admired, and Prescott, of course, was the make of my favorite firearm.

Mickey Free soon regarded me with affection bordering on adulation. Probably I was the first Southern gentlemen he had met, and certainly one of the few *gringos* who treated him as other than a visually impaired illiterate half-breed. Predatory bastards such as my brother Joseph would no doubt have taken evil advantage of young Mickey's fond attachment and transformed him into their personal fancy boy, but I harbored no predilections of this nature. And, truly, once I had introduced him to a couple of *señoritas* who were superb and experienced teachers, it was difficult for him to concentrate on his lessons from me in the skilled use of firearms. Even the indomitable Apaches had not taught him everything.

Over the next few weeks Mickey's proficiency with firearms and women improved remarkably, talents essential to enjoy a long and happy life. His lifelong sensitivity and fear of rejection because of his eye patch soon disappeared, since women, for reasons known only to their sex, found it singularly attractive and somewhat of an aphrodisiac.

After I received the long-awaited telegram from dear Aunt Cordelia informing me of the interment of John Wilkes Booth's "body" in a Baltimore cemetery with attendant publicity of the event, Mickey and I prepared to leave Chihuahua.

CHAPTER THIRTEEN

A brief demonstration of our expertise with weapons and Mickey's linguistic abilities afforded us instant employment with a wagon train bound for El Fortin del Cibolo, Milton Faver's massive fortress on Cibolo Creek across the Río Grande in Texas. I purchased a hand-crafted telescope sight for my Henry and outfitted Mickey with a similar weapon. He had become a fine shot with pistol and rifle and was rapidly mastering the technique of a fast draw, but much preferred the use of a rifle. No doubt these newly acquired skills would prove indispensable, for our route would wind through a merciless desert of sparse vegetation and infrequent watering holes, inhabited by lizards, rattlesnakes, and hostile Apaches.

Our heavily laden wagons crawled at a maddeningly slow pace despite constant urging of the draft animals by apprehensive teamsters. Only a few days out of Chihuahua, I glimpsed the ominous distant flashes of signal mirrors. Already our caravan was being tracked, presumably by Apaches preparing the site and time of their ambush.

Each morning, Mickey and I would ride far out ahead of our wagons on either side of the intended route, then circle back along the flanks and bring up the rear. Day after miserable day we returned without sighting another human being. During each struggle of the wagons through a deep arroyo where they were most vulnerable, we would position ourselves well lateral to the gulch and scan the horizons. The tedium was unremitting, interrupted only by enforced halts to repair broken wagons or harness. These tasks were accomplished with alacrity for during such necessary pauses we felt most at risk. Still nothing, as one dusty, anxious day blended into another.

A week passed, then two. We were only a day or so southwest of Ojinaga and safety when the inevitable occurred.

Shortly after dawn, Mickey and I had ridden out on opposite sides to the rim of the deep gulch containing our wagons. I turned to see if the caravan had begun moving just as twenty or more Apache warriors erupted from the soil like dusty volcanoes in front of our lead wagon. They tore protective wrappings from their carbines and advanced in a ragged line, firing as they came. Oxen and mules screamed piteously as the cartridges ripped into them. The wounded animals heaved convulsively to free themselves from the traces and overturned the lead wagon. The arroyo was too narrow to permit the remaining wagons to form a defensive circle or turn to retreat. The drovers leaped from the wagons and fled for their lives, but two were riddled to a bloody mess before they could leave their seats.

I snatched the Henry from its scabbard and flattened myself on the cañon rim. Through the telescopic sight it seemed as though I was in the midst of the marauders, and I could see vividly each man's expression as my bullets ended his life. When I paused to reload, only two Apaches remained alive. Mickey had been firing slowly and accurately from his side of the gulch. I felt a surge of pride in my young student as I rose to my feet and dispatched the pair of retreating Indians with my revolver.

The din of my shots had scarcely died when I heard and saw Mickey firing across the prairie to the west. I steadied the Henry on a scrub tree and fixed his targets through my telescope. At least a dozen Apache warriors galloped toward us, crouched low over their ponies' necks and almost invisible.

Some time ago Mickey had told me that an Apache without his horse is like a rattlesnake without fangs. Therefore I followed his obvious strategy and assisted my young friend in methodically bringing down every steed. Some of the Indians lay immobile after their fall; others limped or stumbled away in retreat.

Mickey and I mounted and roamed the perimeter executing anything, man or animal, that twitched. To the best of our knowledge nothing survived our reconnaissance. Meanwhile, the effusively grateful drovers buried their two companions, righted the lead wagon and reloaded it, and replaced the dead animals from our remuda. Impatient buzzards already circling would devour everything that remained.

With heightened vigilance and a renewed sense of urgency, our caravan pressed on unmolested to Ojinaga and crossed the Río Grande into Texas without pausing even for a celebratory *cerveza*.

Slightly more than five years after leaving it, I had returned to the country of my birth. Unlike most repatriates, however, I felt neither welcome nor safe.

Crossing the shallow stream which marked the Texas-Mexico border was accomplished without any untoward events, and we embarked on a deeply rutted dusty road that more or less paralleled the silt-laden Río Grande.

Three hard-eyed *vaqueros* in Mr. Faver's employ, dripping with guns and bandoleers of ammunition, joined our procession as guides to our terminus at his fort on Cibolo Creek, a tributary of the Río Grande. It was clear to me that these men were also accompanying us to insure that no one, including members of our party, would be tempted to pilfer anything from the wagons.

While in Chihuahua I had heard several tales of our employer, the legendary Milton Faver, or *Don* Melitón as he was referred to there. With Mickey's able assistance as translator and the *vaqueros'* eagerness to speak of their *patrón*, I surmised a rudimentary biography of this truly remarkable man.

Don Melitón's birth date and place in the States were unknown to them, but as a young man, "less than twenty years", he had fled to Mexico after a dueling incident and for a time had worked in a flour mill not far from the tiny village of Meoqui. Soon after marrying his beloved Francisca, he became a freighter, transporting goods from Meoqui 100 miles north to Ojinaga. This business became so lucrative he extended it south to Chihuahua and north as far as Santa Fé.

Faver accompanied his freighters on many of their trips and shared in the arduous rigors and labor of his employees. On one such expedition he was severely wounded in an assault on his wagons by vicious Apache raiders but recovered after a prolonged convalescence. This episode left him with a profound distaste for any dealings with Indians, peaceful or otherwise.

Eventually his business became so profitable he left it in the care of managers and moved with his family to Ojinaga and opened a general store. Over the next several years, he shrewdly acquired acreage around the only reliable springs in the Chinati Mountain section of the Big Bend area of Texas and established thriving sheep and cattle ranches. To protect his interests from Indian and assorted other two-legged predators, he employed a small army of devoted mercenaries and constructed a huge impregnable fort at

Cibolo Spring. Adjacent to the fort, his laborers built levees, dikes, and an elaborate irrigation system supplying vast fields of vegetables and fruit orchards. His peach brandy was famous throughout the region north and south of the border and was often exchanged for the few items Faver and his men could not grow or make themselves.

With a plentiful supply of food and water, protected by a cadre of intensely loyal *pistoleros*, Faver ruled his fiefdom with absolute authority and meted out his own brand of justice.

Initial probing attacks by Indians not only were easily repelled by Faver's gunmen, but his skilled trackers promptly located any survivors. Their deaths were prolonged and extremely unpleasant. Soon Apaches and Comanches studiously avoided any encroachment on the possessions of *Don* Melitón.

Even the stories of his devoted *pistoleros* had not prepared me for my first sight of Faver's Cibolo Spring headquarters.

In the midst of some of the most remote and god-forsaken territory of the globe, *Don* Melitón had created an oasis of incomparable beauty. Fruit orchards of every variety, particularly peaches, almost surrounded the massive adobe fort. Fields of grain and vegetables meticulously tended by a small army of workers provided amply for the inhabitants of the settlement, and the excess was sold profitably to Army forts and inhabitants of the area. Lofty walls four-feet thick of the fort itself encompassed a courtyard at least 100 square feet bisected by a crystal-clear stream. Circular towers riddled with gun ports anchored the north and south corners, and a ponderous wooden gate, criss-crossed with cast iron, afforded the only entrance. Mounted riflemen patrolled the fields and could be seen in the hills to every horizon.

Don Melitón himself welcomed Mickey and me in English and Spanish, then introduced us to his lovely and gracious wife, Francisca. This alluring vision spoke classic English with a delightfully lilting accent. From her intriguing choice of words, I knew she must be a devotee of Shakespeare's works, suggesting an opportunity for intriguing dialogue between us in the future. Her beauty and singular attractiveness lay not so much in her classic features and svelte figure, but the little gestures—the tilt of her head, roguish glint of her eyes, the secretive smile that foretold unimaginable pleasures. I had not beheld such an enchantress in some years, possibly never.

Milton Faver was the breed of man who always appears much larger than his actual size, with an authoritative voice and imposing bearing that commanded respect and demanded attention. I would judge him to have been in his early fifties when we met, and I liked him immediately. His thick mane of graying hair was forever tousled, and he had a habit of combing his callused fingers through it while talking. Faver spoke Spanish with such ease and fluency that English appeared to be his second language. His seamed visage and coppery complexion testified to his predilection for the outdoor life, although I soon learned he generally preferred to travel by buggy rather than horseback. This was indeed fortunate, since Mrs. Faver rode better than he, I, and most of the *vaqueros*. Her horsemanship was yet another source of pride for her adoring husband.

During the years of my stay with *Don* Melitón and his wife, I never found cause to alter my initial impression that theirs was the most perfect marriage I would ever know.

A brief demonstration of our skills with firearms convinced Mr. Faver to offer Mickey and me permanent employment. The arrangement proved mutually beneficial. In addition to our guard duties we trained Mr. Faver's *pistoleros* to a much higher degree of skill with firearms, and Mickey was particularly useful in bartering with the occasional bands of Indians journeying to and fro across the Río Grande as the seasons changed.

Federal troops were beginning to reoccupy forts in this region abandoned during the war, and their quartermasters visited frequently to negotiate purchases of beef, produce, and fruit. Always the officers were treated to sumptuous banquets hosted by the enchanting Mrs. Faver, and liberal doses of the peach brandy for which Cibolo Creek Ranch was justifiably famous. Somehow a gift flask or two invariably found its way into the saddlebags of the column's commanding officer.

During one such visit Mickey's linguistic abilities and adeptness with firearms so impressed the Federal contingent that he was hired on the spot at a lavish salary to scout for troops attempting to rid the Southwest of despoilers, Indian or otherwise.

I regretted losing the companionship of this young man and his cheerful multilingual banter more than I would care to admit, but had already sensed his impatience with the relatively tranquil life at the fort, and his longing to return to an environment I would have found excruciatingly intolerable. We parted after exchanging solemn vows to accomplish a reunion in the near future, but I never saw Mickey Free again.

As the months passed, I began accompanying Mr. Faver more and more on his frequent trips to inspect his other interests. His cattle ranch at Cienega Spring was protected by a tall stockade with two defense towers, but the sheep ranch at La Morita was less well fortified and had unfortunately suffered a recent devastating raid by a roving band of Apaches. Mr. Faver dispatched me on a punitive expedition at the head of six hardened *pistoleros* led by one of his implacable Apache trackers.

This man, known only as Aguilar, a head shorter than I, trotted slightly ahead of our horses from dawn until dusk for the entire journey. At irregular intervals he would pause momentarily to sniff the air like an animal or examine minutely some inconsequential object he sighted on the ground.

Unerringly as a hound locates the covey, Aguilar led us to our quarry hidden in a box cañon two day's journey from La Morita. After nightfall, Aguilar and one of our gunmen noiselessly strangled the two sentries, then stampeded the Apache horses. In the pandemonium that followed, our rifles snuffed the lives of all that remained, save two who surrendered. These unfortunates would have fared better had they joined their companions in instant death.

Even now, I can not adequately describe details of the scene which followed. Suffice it to say that one man's demise was unmercifully prolonged, excruciatingly painful, excessively gory, and unbearably noisy. The remaining survivor's fate was to relay a visual message to his brethren who might consider another foray into the land of *Don Melitón*. Therefore his mutilation was limited to the unhurried hacking removal of ears, nose, tongue, and genitals. The initials **DM** were seared into his back with a hot iron then used to cauterize excessive bleeding from his ragged wounds.

From the time of this incident until I left the employ of Mr. Faver, I do not recall any additional visitations by Apaches.

I had thought that the antecedent polymorphous scenes

of carnage I had witnessed or participated in would certainly have inured my emotions to any further trauma, but I was wrong. This recent ghastly business sickened me, and with considerable effort I forced my brain to focus on more pleasurable thoughts.

No healing vision or thought I could summon could possibly be more satisfying than sensual images of the lovely Francisca. Such fantasies suffused my consciousness with blissful relief during the long ride back to Cibolo.

Don Melitón, I was informed on arrival, would be in Ojinaga for two more days, and I was to give my report on the expedition to *la patrona Faver* at dinner that evening.

Like an eager schoolboy I scrubbed my skin until it shone, shaved carefully, and dressed in my most suitable outfit. The afternoon hours plodded endlessly, although I immersed myself in a dog-eared copy of *Hamlet* and refreshed my memory of its ageless lines. A suitor prepared is a suitor rewarded.

An impassive liveried servant ushered me into the dim paneled study illuminated by wrought iron candelabras. When she rose to greet me, flickering shadows accentuated the ethereal loveliness of the incomparable Francisca. As I bowed and brushed my lips over her outstretched hand, I could sense a fine tremor of anticipation.

After we were seated and served our drinks, I described with considerable restraint and delicacy the results of our recent mission. Our conversation was rather formal and stilted until after the second brandy, and we had adjourned to a spacious dining salon crowned by a cathedral ceiling. Francisca and I sat at opposite ends of an ornately carved wooden table so massive it must have been assembled in the room.

During the meal I cleverly manipulated our conversation

from mundane polite topics to Francisca's interest in Shakespeare. She had originally begun her study of the bard in order to improve her English but continued to read his works, savoring the majesty of his words and the intricate excitement of his plots. I modestly confessed a similar interest and shyly inquired if she would care to hear a recitation.

I am sure she agreed out of sheer politeness, but, as I rose and began to declaim the familiar soliloquies, her face was a mask of pure rapture.

While I progressed through favorite selections from my vast repertoire, she laughed; she wept; she was entranced. It was truly the greatest performance of my career. I ended with a deep bow, and, before I was fully erect, Francisca unexpectedly enveloped me in an impassioned embrace. I knew at that moment she was mine.

Shocked at her impulsiveness, Francisca suddenly released me and stepped back, blushing most becomingly. I ached to hold her again, but the image of a bloody torso emblazoned with the brand **DM** invaded my brain. Only my superb thespian skills permitted me to suppress my raging passion and coolly thank Francisca for a delightful evening. I gently kissed her hand, bade her good night, and dejectedly returned to my quarters.

I pummeled my pillow into a lumpy mass until I regained control of my pent-up emotions and fell asleep at last. Intensely erotic dreams disturbed my rest, followed by prolonged episodes of wakefulness as I contemplated recent events and alternatives for the future. Dawn arrived with my ambivalence still unresolved.

Mr. Faver returned later that day and almost immediately isolated himself until dusk with his sensuous wife. I could only imagine his pleasures while I patrolled the perimeter of the ranch as was my duty. That evening I was summoned to Mr. Faver's study for a glass of brandy and his thanks for the successful prosecution of my mission to "reprimand", as he put it, the Apache raiders.

He had been equally successful in his business endeavors, having obtained a long-term contract with the Federal government to supply foodstuffs to its forts, and had appreciably expanded his holdings by acquiring additional acreage and water rights.

He had also researched documents in Ojinaga which had convinced him that the silver mines near Cibolo, long ago abandoned by the Spanish, warranted investigation as soon as he had obtained the proper lease agreements.

I could not help but admire this man who possessed boundless energy and enthusiasm for life and its opportunities for men of vision. Like a skilled professional juggler, he could maintain any number of objectives in motion simultaneously with untrammeled ease.

Such feelings, however, in no way diminished my unendurable lust for his precious wife; therefore, I accepted with alacrity his invitation to accompany them on a javelina hunt as body guard and participant.

We ventured into mountains to the east of the fort near the Big Bend of the Río Grande accompanied by an entourage of servants driving wagons containing every creature comfort. I rode with Mr. Faver in his buggy while Francisca raced ahead on her gelding.

Our first night in camp I slept little, disturbed not so much by unaccustomed animal sounds from the adjacent crags and cañons, but those emanating from the nearby tent of Mr. and Mrs. Faver.

Shortly before sunrise he and I left to enter our blinds and await the arrival of our quarry. Francisca had mumbled that she would remain in camp to bathe.

Faver concealed himself in a clump of brush below an outcropping of shale near a well-worn track. I ascended a slight rise behind and to the left of him as the first coruscation of dawn appeared.

As I stared intently at the path in front of us, a flicker of motion appeared on the verge of my peripheral vision. I turned my head and initially saw nothing. Then, as I squinted, it was there.

Creeping silently across the shale, a sinuous tawny panther was stalking Mr. Faver. In that one split second I considered my alternatives. I could do nothing. The immense animal would devour Mr. Faver. I could shoot Faver, claiming a tragic accident, or I could kill the beast.

I fired.

The animal fell dead, almost lacerating Mr. Faver in its death throes. I raced to his side expecting to find the man quivering with relief, but Faver was icily calm. He shook my hand and thanked me for saving his life as if we had just concluded a business transaction. Then he dismissed me to return to our camp and bring up his buggy so he could transport his panther to be skinned. Typically the man was determined to remain until he had completed the day's hunt to his satisfaction.

All the servants were busy at the spring nearby when I rode in, and Francisca poked her dripping head out of the tent to inquire about the shot she had heard. When I explained the recent happenings, she opened the tent flap wide and stood in the opening naked and lovely as a Greek statue, the vision of my restless nights. In a husky voice I can still hear, Francisca offered to reward me most generously for saving her husband's life.

Children will often prance about a campfire, tossing in

branches to see the flames mount higher and higher. Closer and closer they venture, stirring the red-hot coals and squealing with delight as the sparks soar. Their excitement soon exceeds caution and a horrible tragedy occurs. The unending sorrow that invariably follows is all the more bitter because such a catastrophe was so unnecessary.

There had been and would be many women for me, while I had only one life to lose. And I had been a fugitive for nearly eight years. I had no desire to continue fleeing, especially from the relentless and implacable trackers of *Don* Melitón.

I bowed graciously in a gesture of appreciation and expressed my thanks. With masterful self-control and deep regret, I declined her offer. She smiled enigmatically and murmured—"Then we shall remain friends."—and closed the flap.

My conscience dictates that I should record that my actions were based less on loyalty to *Don* Melitón than images of his vengeance. No conquest, even Francisca, is worth that risk. For once in my life my instinct of self-preservation overcame my lust.

I had made my decision and, shortly after we returned from the excursion to Cibolo Fort, informed Mr. Faver that I would soon leave, for my restless spirit had returned. He understood this logic with impressive clarity, as he had observed it often in his young *vaqueros* and, I suspect, in himself. Business-like as always, he thanked me formally and, despite my protestations, insisted on presenting me with a far larger purse than I expected. Francisca, accomplished actress to the end, bid me a gracious but reserved farewell, smiling politely as I gently kissed her hand.

My friends, the *vaqueros*, were much more demonstrative. These tough young men waved their sombreros in the air and exuberantly fired the weapons I had trained them so diligently to use. Their cries of—"*¡Vaya con Dios, amigo!*"—reverberated in my ears as I mounted Corazón, unfurled my umbrella, and began another journey.

That night, as I unpacked a saddlebag to prepare my camp, I found the book. On the flyleaf of a small volume of quotations from Shakespeare was inscribed in a feathery hand: **Thank you for all you did for us—and what you did not do. Francisca.**

CHAPTER FOURTEEN

I had been warned repeatedly of the dangers facing anyone traveling alone through West Texas but chose to ignore these ominous admonitions. I had far rather experience a quick death at the hands of Indians or bandits than endure the prolonged agonies of stagecoach travel and the terminal affliction of fatally boring conversation from fellow passengers.

With Corazón trailing a sometimes balky pack mule, we made excellent progress, and I relished the occasional opportunity to obtain a hot bath and change in diet afforded by periodic respites at small inns or stagecoach stops although the prices charged for such meager services were uniformly outrageous.

Without having encountered any untoward events on the trail thus far, I paused for a few days at Comanche Springs, a truly amazing flow of water in this otherwise scenically deprived land. From thence I headed northeast and crossed the well-defined trail followed by marauding Comanches on their annual forays into Mexico. But I encountered not a single Indian on my trek from Comanche Springs to the junction of the Concho Rivers near the cavalry post of Fort Concho.

Santa Angela, the parasitic town across the river from this immaculate encampment, I remember as a hodge-podge collection of shacks housing dispensers of toxic whiskey and grimy prostitutes so repulsive they should have returned their truly desperate customers' payments with interest. I did not tarry long in this foul hell-hole and continued my journey northeast, intending to reach the burgeoning city of Dallas.

There I would consolidate my funds from banks in Canada, my oil investments in Pennsylvania, and the legacy from my benefactor in Java. With the considerable sum then available, I planned to invest a portion and live comfortably on the remainder. I had my fill of traveling, particularly by horseback or stagecoach, and wished to begin a new chapter in my life.

I abandoned my rôle as the gunman, Wade Prescott, on the journey from Cibola, allowed my cropped hair to grow to its accustomed length, and chose the alias John St. Helen. I have no idea where this name came from. It popped into my head while I was riding through a rather featureless landscape, and I immediately fancied the sound of it. My cherished umbrella was tattered and broken to the extent I could repair it no longer. Finally I was compelled to discard it with the regret one feels on leaving an old friend. As soon as possible after arriving in Dallas, I would purchase a new wardrobe to complete my transformation from *pistolero* to prosperous businessman.

But my well-laid plans went awry in a fashion I could have never predicted. Intrigued by a sequence of posters touting the efficacy of healing mineral waters in the tiny settlement of Glen Rose Mill, I decided to obtain a few nights' rest from the saddle. I unpacked my belongings in a combination hotel-saloon which appeared surprisingly clean and offered a marginally better menu than the usual bleak tasteless fare available at such establishments.

I soon learned that an additional source of civic pride in Glen Rose was the potency of distilled beverages manufactured by rustic entrepreneurs in the surrounding forests.

Perhaps it was the mineral water which accounted for their product's reputation, but, after a hesitant sampling, I was of the opinion its taste was more likely a result of these waters leaching through the ossuary of dinosaur bones permeating the limestone deposits in this region. Such whiskey's deficiency in taste was more than adequately compensated by its marginally sub-lethal potency.

For over a week I soaked in the baths, ate well, and practiced my firearms well away from the village after I had assured myself I was not being observed. Although I did not wish my skills to become rusty, discretion in their use would be a staple of my new persona.

As time passed, I gradually developed a reasonable tolerance for the local bottled poison but restricted my intake to minimum daily requirements. Each evening I joined the only entertainment in town, a poker game at the inn. Most of the participants thereof possessed the intellectual capacity of three-toed sloths. These mental giants had learned to count slowly the spots on the cards, moving their lips with each number, and could usually recognize the face cards after some cogitation.

Following this agonizing period of identification these simple souls bet outrageously on any two cards that remotely resembled each other. Their stupid play was my sole entertainment and I felt obligated to return the favor by intentionally losing small sums to these donkeys who brayed contentedly.

But one player, W. W. Snider, who could count slightly faster than his companions and thus fancied himself superior to all present, began to nettle me. His bleating laughter and annoying habit of belittling other players became tiresome. I suspected Snider's initials stood for "Without Wisdom", and I had learned he was the owner of the inn.

Thus he could afford to suffer financial setbacks much easier than his associates.

I set my trap carefully. Over the course of successive evenings, I began losing progressively larger sums to Snider, taking care that I won only small pots. This dolt could have never become an actor. His transparent facial expressions and body language precisely revealed the strength of each hand dealt to him, and the weakness of his bluffs. After several nights of careful baiting, it was time for his dénouement.

Five-card stud, a man's game, was no place for fools. I waited until I was sure I had him, then pounced. Although I proffered him several opportunities to fold and save himself, his greed and bluster overcame him. He continued to raise bet after bet. When the hole card was finally turned, I became the proud owner of his saloon.

I ignored his curses and threats for a moment, then silenced them with the lightning insertion of the Prescott's barrel into his foul mouth.

As I have said before, anything worth doing is worth doing to excess. I therefore decided travelers and visitors to the mineral waters and dinosaur bones of this area deserved better accommodations. Sparing no expense, I completely renovated the Healing Waters Saloon, changing everything but the name. The Carrera family, all superb cooks, was hired, and almost overnight each meal was seated to capacity. Sam Marston, a colored bartender of impressive size with an encyclopedic knowledge of alcoholic potions, was equipped with an excellent selection of wines, beer, and whiskies, as well as a truncated 10-gauge shotgun. For the mundane tastes of those more concerned with quantity than quality we continued to provide the local vintage. Our beds and rooms were kept meticulously clean by the younger

Carreras, and every conceivable amenity was provided for our guests, save one. Those seeking soiled doves must look elsewhere. I harbored no dislike for these ladies, but an abiding contempt for their usual customers.

I paid my employees outrageous salaries, left them alone to manage day to day affairs at the inn, and found them to be marvelously efficient and intensely loyal.

Money poured in, far beyond my expectations, and in a few short months my investment had been returned many times over. This bonanza I shared generously with my employees, for truly I had no need of additional wealth. The success of my inn and the increased number of visitors to our little community naturally earned for me the plaudits of local businessmen to the extent that I was asked to be master of ceremonies at the July 4th celebration in Glen Rose. Also appearing on the dais would be General J. M. Taylor of Seminole War fame, and a young attorney, Finis Bates, from the nearby town of Granbury.

After lengthy and rather sonorous speeches by these two gentlemen, I was asked to say a few words. Fortified by an unusually large intake of brandy on that festive day, I delivered a short, eloquent discourse on the vast opportunities for successful enterprise in our great nation. My peroration was received with enthusiastic applause, far greater than the response offered to my predecessors. This recognition seemed to vex the old general but earned an invitation from Bates to join him for a drink. Of course one did not suffice, and I spent an enjoyable afternoon with this ambitious and articulate young attorney, little realizing that I would soon require his professional services.

The monumentally stupid and malicious Mr. Snider had failed to renew or obtain a license for the sale of tobacco and whiskey while operating his inn. When confronted with a possible indictment and arrest on these charges, he promptly shifted the blame to me, falsely claiming that I was aware of the discrepancy and had not filed the proper documents.

To deny such charges, even under oath, would have meant an issue of my word against Snider's and most certainly necessitate my appearance in court. Although the charges were patently ridiculous, I wished to avoid any involvement with government officials for obvious reasons.

I therefore turned the matter over to Finis Bates, and was greatly impressed with the young lawyer's efficiency in settling the matter promptly and satisfactorily out of court. His fee was quite reasonable and during the management of this unpleasantness we became fast friends.

Less than a month later, Mr. Snider's body was found in the woods near Granbury, apparently the victim of a tragic hunting accident. Briefly a cloud of suspicion descended about me, but the sworn testimony of my loyal employees as to my presence in the Healing Waters at the time of Snider's misfortune absolved me completely.

The inn continued to prosper, requiring the enlargement of our kitchen and dining areas and the addition of several more bedrooms. I was convinced such establishments offering clean, comfortable lodgings, a variety of savory foods, and equally well managed adjacent livery stables would be instantly successful across the land.

America was on the move after the rigors of war. Passenger travel by rail was rapidly supplanting the slow, uncomfortable stagecoach, while freight and mail shipments were already transported more efficiently and expeditiously by trains. In my opinion a fortune was waiting for those providing restful accommodations at a reasonable price for the new generation of transients.

Finis and I had discussed over many hours and many glasses my idea of a chain of such facilities. He was preparing the legal documents for such a venture and I was consolidating my finances when the slippery finger of fate targeted me once again.

In the spring of 1873 I began to experience the gradual onset of a vague malaise. My much-envied vigor had waned, and I required a conscious effort to perform daily tasks previously accomplished almost automatically. My appetite diminished, soon followed by a singular loss of interest in the pending financial ventures, my practice with firearms, and even my afternoon tots of brandy. I began to retire earlier than usual but still awoke unrefreshed. As the days passed, I experienced fevers followed by drenching sweats especially at night, and rapidly became so weak I was confined to bed.

Unbeknownst to me, faithful Sam had sent word to Finis of my malady, and a doctor of his acquaintance in Granbury was dispatched to see me. By the time he arrived, my fevers and chills had become unremitting and I recall splitting headaches along with the development of an evanescent scarlet rash over my entire body.

This porcine physician grunted, poked, and prodded in a desultory fashion, prescribed a purgative, pronounced my condition to be in God's hands, and levied an outrageous fee. Soon after his departure, I became delusional, and learned of the following events after my recovery.

Sam or one of the Carreras lingered at my bedside day and night, cooling my fevers and tending my needs while I writhed and shook with ague. In desperation, *Señora* Carrera sent for a *curandera,* a Mexican folk healer, to work her magic. This aged crone chanted eerie incantations around my bed, and performed the ritual of *barriendo,* sweeping an intact egg over my body, then cracking the egg in a saucer left under the bed overnight. Next morning she announced she could see an eye in the yolk, and that I was cured of the *mal ojo* (evil eye).

Whether this mumbo-jumbo played any part in the recovery I do not know, but within hours my fever had broken, my senses had returned, and I was recuperating. In a few days I was up and about, albeit limp as a noodle.

While I was resting in my room one afternoon, Finis dropped by to speed my recovery with a flask of excellent brandy, but I could tolerate only a few tentative sips.

Although I had no recall whatsoever of a previous visit, Finis had sat by my bedside one afternoon while Sam and the Carreras were attending customers. He smiled, then laughed aloud as he recalled for me some of my ravings.

Apparently I had recited numerous selections from Shakespeare, called repeatedly for "someone named Francisca" and then, Finis chuckled and leaned toward me conspiratorially. "You said you were really John Wilkes Booth, and mumbled something like Roby, or Robby's dead, not me. Then you called out repeatedly for someone named Davy, and wept. Whatever illness you had, my friend, it certainly fired your imagination."

Only my masterful skill as an actor prevented the shock and foreboding I felt from registering on my face. After all my travels and disguises I had blurted out the truth in an unguarded moment. To allay any suspicions, I forced myself to laugh with Bates.

After the passage of a sufficient period of time in desultory conversation, I asked in an off-hand manner that he not reveal my ravings to anyone. I suggested that such revelations would be embarrassing to say the least, and might cause some deranged Lincolnophile to do me harm. Finis laughed with me and swore to keep my secret.

Perhaps my weakened condition was partially responsible, but I continued to be plagued with unreasonable fears that my identity was no longer a secret and my life was in peril. I again sought the legal services of my friend, Finis Bates, stating I wished to reward those who had nursed me so assiduously to health, and my proximate brush with death had affected me with an abiding longing for a reunion with my family in Kentucky.

With one stroke of a pen I deeded Healing Waters Inn and a considerable sum for operating expenses to Sam Marston and the Carrera family "for services rendered". Finis would deliver the document after my departure.

I said *"Adiós"* to my friend and promised to contact him after I had gone east to Kentucky, then mounted Corazón in the dead of night and headed west for parts unknown.

CHAPTER FIFTEEN

West Texas has been aptly described as a land where everything either bites, stings, scratches, or breaks your heart. On my sojourn from the Mexican border, I had found nothing to dispute that succinct appraisal and had no desire to explore the matter further. Therefore, soon after leaving my friends at Glen Rose and Granbury, I turned Corazón's head due north and soon had crossed the Brazos River.

As I rode through the rather dull landscape, my thoughts wandered back to my recent illness. Would Finis Bates consider the untimely revelation of my true identity as a febrile hallucination, or would he become suspicious enough to investigate the matter further? Regardless of his decision, my most propitious strategy was to continue my present course leading to the most indomitable refuge in the land for those who wished to "disappear"—Indian Territory.

In the mid-1830s tribes were forcibly uprooted from their ancestral lands in the Southeast and marched to this arid, flat, and unwanted region. Many perished *en route;* subsequent generations struggled to survive by their own valiant efforts and meager government subsidies. As the years passed, tribes from the Great Plains, primarily Kiowas, Comanches, and Apaches, were herded and corralled in the Territory. Tribal councils performed administrative duties, and the area was lackadaisically patrolled by inept Indian police.

Desperate situations begat desperados, Indian and white. These brigands rushed to exploit tribal frictions, apathy of the Federal government, and total absence of any effective law enforcement. Vigilantes roamed the land, ruling by the profligate use of lead and hemp. For an honest man of principles the Territory was an outpost of hell. For those adept with cards and guns it was a slice of heaven. During the summer and early autumn of 1873, my life was positively angelic.

Winning cards seemed to come my way, and I was careful to keep moving from settlement to settlement, avoiding as much as possible the clumsy attempts of disappointed losers to recoup their losses with firearms. To the best of my recollection, I found it necessary to kill only three—or was it five?—malcontents during my time in the Territory, all in self-defense, of course. Two, I recall, unwisely accused me of cheating, and one idiot would not cease turning over discards after repeated warnings.

But my time was not entirely spent in gambling and mayhem. While staying at an inn near the Canadian River, the Sioux proprietor, Black Owl, instructed me in the rudiments of his language. I must confess I entered into this study only because of my fascination with phonetics, and never anticipated any practical application. The future would prove me wrong. In return for Black Owl's tutelage, I enhanced his rudimentary skills in poker and faro to a level approaching my own.

My previous experiences with Indians, as I have chronicled, had almost invariably been violent in the extreme. But my friendship with Black Owl, and many others while I was in the Territory, completely changed my perspective. There were bad elements to be sure, just as in all of us, and many were not the "noble savages" of James Fenimore Cooper's nauseating drivel. In fact, one of the card cheats I shot was an Indian.

However, the vast majority of my new friends were the most resilient people I had known, and had suffered more indignities, generation after generation, at the hands of our nefarious Washington bureaucrats than any people on earth. Torn from their homelands, forced to live on an inadequate dole, and treated like vermin, these native Americans had somehow managed to retain their pride, their honor, and their innate sense of decency. But how long could these admirable qualities persist under the program of callous benign neglect foisted upon them by incompetents in Washington?

Not content with breaking treaties, stealing Indian lands, and forced emigration of its residents to pestilential reservations, the Federal government seemed bent on pursuing a policy of absolute intentional genocide, a policy more vicious than the vindictive desecration of the South by carpetbaggers and scalawags.

General Custer's massacre of peaceful Indians, women, and babies at the Washita River a few years past was trumpeted in the Northern newspapers as a "great victory". And the policy of "the only good Indian is a dead Indian" seemed to be the catch phrase of the nation.

So many conflicts and tragedies of the future could have been avoided by honesty and fair dealing, but such a policy was incompatible with a nation so obsessed with its "manifest destiny" that all who opposed it were trampled to dust.

I whiled away the long winter months in the pleasant company of Black Owl and his family. There I continued his detailed education in the probabilities and percentages involved in games of chance that would afford him a steady income from the far less skilled patrons of his establishment. We foraged for game throughout the prairie that surrounded us, and, under Black Owl's instruction, I acquired skills second nature to the Sioux, but mastered by few whites. By spring, with only minimal application of make-up, I could easily pass as an Indian, possessing talents of incomparable value for survival in my future travels.

It was time for me to move on. Many times during the past winter, travelers regaled our poker games with rumors of gold in the Dakota Territory, and I had entertained the notion of journeying to that area. I had no desire to grub in the earth seeking the elusive nuggets and flakes, but intended to mine the far richer lode of fools and their money. I have never fully understood the compulsion of those with limited intellect to squander their meager fortunes, earned through incredible hardship, in games of chance. Games in which they possessed only rudimentary knowledge of the rules, no conception of percentages and odds, forced to rely on sheer luck to achieve any gains. Sometimes I almost regretted fleecing these poor sheep, but no one forced them to play, and life is replete with painful lessons to be learned.

I saddled Corazón and obtained a pack mule for one final hunt to last several days. Black Owl's larder would be well stocked in partial payment for his and his family's innumerable courtesies to me during my pleasant winter's respite.

My hunt was eminently successful. The mule was laden with four-legged and winged game, enough for many feasts to come, and I expected a joyous welcome. But the inn was silent. Pistol in hand, I entered a scene of utter chaos.

Broken dishes and overturned furniture littered the room. A crimson trail of blood led to the partially opened kitchen door. As I moved cautiously through the débris, I was startled by a yelp of relief from Black Owl's wife who cowered behind the door.

"I thought they were coming back to kill us all," she sobbed. "They hurt Black Owl bad."

I holstered my Prescott at the sound of her voice and followed her into the kitchen. Black Owl lay immobile on a pallet near the fireplace wrapped in a bloody blanket. His young son knelt, weeping, at his side. My examination was quick but thorough. He was barely conscious, obviously beaten savagely over his head and face, particularly on the left side. A deep gash, still oozing blood, extended from his left shoulder across his chest to his breastbone. But the wound had not punctured the chest cavity and did not appear mortal.

I attempted to soothe the weeping boy and busied him restarting the fire. While I tore the blanket into strips to pack and bind Black Owl's chest wound, his wife haltingly related the atrocity visited upon her hapless family.

Before noon that day, three buffalo hunters had stormed into the inn, cursing and demanding whiskey. She and her son huddled in the kitchen while Black Owl explained that no whiskey was allowed on the reservation. They continued to berate him, then shoved him aside and began a ruthless search, overturning chairs and tables. Finding nothing, they became enraged. The two smaller men watched and laughed while the huge third man pummeled Black Owl mercilessly with his fists. Black Owl refused to fight back; then the man slashed him with a skinning knife and clubbed him insensible with the butt of his revolver.

The three left, still laughing, mounted their horses, and headed north.

A raging fury almost superseded my better judgment, for I longed to ride down these sadistic miscreants forthwith and dispense my own brand of justice. But reason dictated I must tend to the needs of Black Owl and his family and postpone my day of reckoning.

Over the next three days and long nights we watched my friend gradually regain his senses. Eventually he was able to sip broth and gruel, there was no further bleeding from his chest wound, and he spoke rationally. However, I suspected he would never recover vision in his left eye.

I tarried at Black Owl's inn until he was up and about, albeit painfully, and provided his wife with funds sufficient that the government doctor would minister to Black Owl regularly, and obtain consultation if necessary for treatment of his severely damaged left eye.

My benevolent mien extended only to my friend and his family, however, for I raged inwardly at this recent episode which typified the inhuman treatment of Indians by their oppressors, who most often went unpunished. I could do little to change the genocidal policies of the Federals, but I would certainly pursue my personal vendetta against those who had so gleefully violated my friend and his home without cause.

Let the law be damned! I would be the judge and jury, my Prescott would be the executioner.

Black Owl and his wife had provided a fair description of the three men, buffalo hunters all from their appearance and smell. Two were small with narrow faces, "like weasels," Black Owl had said. One had a cocked eye, the other a high-pitched voice, "like a woman." The third a hulking, bearded brute who resembled the beasts he sought, and was missing most of the index and middle fingers of his left hand. Even a tracker much less adept than I should be able to find these worthies and distinguish them from their equally repulsive and odiferous colleagues.

Black Owl's wife had heard one of them yell—"On to Kansas!"—as they rode off, so I would head northwest, following their tracks as long as possible.

Until the rains came as I neared the Kansas border, a blind man could have followed the hoof prints, cold campfires, and dead animals left in the wake of my quarry. They slaughtered buffalo just for the tongues, antelope for just one haunch, and many animals just to satisfy their perverted joy of killing.

In Kansas, their trail led though every saloon in every settlement large enough to support a tavern. My search for the scurrilous trio was rendered even easier by the invariable information from bartenders. "If you're looking for buffalo hunters, head for Buffalo City at the railhead. So many there you can 'most smell 'em from here."

Buffalo City, formerly a drab collection of dug-outs, tents, and sod huts, blossomed overnight after the Atchison, Topeka, and Santa Fé railroad reached there in 1872. Renamed Dodge City for Fort Dodge, a nearby Army post, it promptly became a lawless pesthole. At least fifteen men were killed in the first year of its existence.

Bands of vigilantes roamed the streets, dispensing their nebulous brand of justice by the strength of their mobs. In the summer of 1873, vigilantes killed one William Taylor, a servant of Colonel Richard Dodge, commander of the fort. Dodge wired the governor of Kansas who ordered troops to the community. A semblance of order was restored by the troops and the appointment of an honest man, Charles Bassett, as sheriff.

Swarms of buffalo hunters, each earning over $100 a day, flocked to the settlement and into the welcoming arms of gamblers, soiled doves, and assorted blackguards who profited mightily from the appalling slaughter of the buffalo.

From 1872 to 1874 over 850,000 hides were shipped

from Dodge City alone, and, in three years, more than 3,000,000 buffalo were exterminated from the plains.

In Dodge City of the mid-1870s, life was cheap, human or buffalo. In the early summer of 1874, I rode into this vermin-infested pesthole alone.

It was as if I had entered a human ant nest. Frenzied construction of wooden frame buildings continued day and night, but much of the populace lived, drank, gambled, and fornicated in tents, sod huts, or in the open. The streets were hoof-deep morasses of mud and animal waste, clouds of insects clogged the nostrils of animals and humans, and the wind blew unceasingly. But surpassing all other sensory assaults was the almost palpable unforgettable odor of human sweat, assorted animals, feces, and mountainous stacks of putrefying buffalo hides. I smelled the city long before I could see it, and vowed I would take care of business promptly and put this hell-hole behind me as soon as possible.

Fortunately I was able to secure a reasonably clean room in one of the wooden hotels and, with further financial inducement, a soothing hot bath.

Money not only talks, it induces others to speak. In less than a week of rewarding several enterprising bartenders for their co-operation, I had located my three hunters. Now they would be the hunted.

I was informed the trio was leaving Dodge the following morning for another lucrative assault on the defenseless buffalo. At a respectful distance from their wagons I followed their lumbering progress over the rolling prairie hills to the site of their first night's camp. I had no desire to spend any more time than necessary away from the comfort of my hotel, so, as soon as they squatted by their fire eating whatever such beasts eat, I crept closer.

Skills learned from my Sioux friends served me well, for I was soon at the verge of the campfire's glow, undetected. I rose, Prescott in hand, and, before they could react, executed each one with a precise shot to the forehead. They did not so much as twitch.

Without a backward glance I walked back to Corazón, mounted, and cantered back to Dodge.

At least buffalo retain some value after they are killed, if only for the price of their hides. These three bastards were completely worthless, alive or dead.

I never knew the names of these barbarians, but seldom has a killing afforded me so much satisfaction.

CHAPTER SIXTEEN

Prior to retiring after this day's good work, I tarried in the hotel's miniscule barroom to absorb the warming effects of a passable whiskey and the animated conversation of its regular occupants.

As usual, the ongoing discussion involved General George Armstrong Custer's announcement of the discovery of gold in the Dakota Territory, and the illegal stampede of fortune hunters into these sacred lands of the Lakota Sioux.

Although a treaty signed at Fort Laramie in 1868 required the Federal government and its troops to protect these lands from white invaders, over 1,200 soldiers under the command of the infamous General Custer were instead protecting the intruders from the betrayed and beleaguered Sioux.

In the summer of 1874, Custer's military expedition was mobilized to locate a suitable site for constructing a fort in the Black Hills. As soon as rumors of gold strikes in the very hills he was to explore reached Custer, he hired professional miners to accompany his military force. When these men did locate the precious yellow metal in abundance, the news spread like a cancer. The trickle of whites into the supposedly inviolate lands of the Sioux became a torrent.

Many Sioux left their homes and fled west to unceded land in the Territory of Montana. Others resisted in a futile struggle against overwhelming odds.

In 1875, officials of the Grant administration came under considerable pressure to purchase the rich lands owned by peaceful Lakota Sioux "agency Indians", but the tribes refused to sell. The government then decided to corral the roving bands of Indians harassing the white invaders and force them into newly designated reservations comprised of land on which gold had not been discovered.

In December, 1875, messages were sent to the roaming tribes warning them to move immediately to the new enclaves, or be officially designated as "hostiles" by the U.S. War Department.

Wrongs which were borne in silence by many Indians would have surely precipitated unparalleled acts of violence if such indignities were suffered by their oppressors. But some of the aggrieved tribesmen did speak eloquently of their grievances.

One Lakota chief greeted the government negotiators with: "I am glad to see you, my friends, but I hear you have come to move us again. Tell your people that since the Great Father promised that we should never be removed, we have been moved five times. I think you had better put the Indians on wheels and you can run them around wherever you wish."

The Sioux leader, Sitting Bull, would not meet with officials sent to him, but conveyed this message: "Whenever you have found a white man who will tell the truth, you may return and I shall be glad to negotiate with you."

To the whites with vested interests in Indian lands, as with many Northerners, General Custer was an intrepid hero of the recent war and noble protector of settlers from marauding savage Indians.

But if the truth would be known, he was a flamboyant and egotistical commander of troops in the War Between the States, whose reckless charges resulted in needless slaughter of his men.

However, his battlefield aggression was appreciatively noted by his commanding generals, particularly General Phillip Sheridan.

After the war, Custer was appointed lieutenant-colonel of the 7th Cavalry and led his troopers in an ineffectual campaign against the southern Cheyennes. He followed this débacle by being court-martialed and suspended from service for a year, charged with unauthorized absence from duty. Only through the intercession of his old friend General Sheridan was he restored to command in 1868.

In the eyes of those who averred that "the only good Indian is a dead Indian," Custer redeemed himself by ordering the massacre of men, women, and children of Black Kettle's settlement encamped on the Washita River in November, 1868. These peaceable Sioux were *en route* to assigned reservations when attacked and slaughtered by Custer and his men.

Custer professed to hate all Indians as much as his commanders, Generals Sheridan and Sherman. He was also very fond of trumpeting his undying love beyond measure for his wife Libby. But the hypocrisy of this man was typified by his kidnapping of a beautiful, seventeen-year-old Sioux maiden, Monaseetah, after the Washita massacre, ostensibly to serve as his "interpreter". However, the girl spoke not a word of English. Somehow, communication was effected for she bore him a fair-skinned papoose, Yellow Bird.

This poseur was the saintly, long-haired hero in command of a motley collection of troopers largely composed of immigrant Irish and Germans empowered to wrest the gold-bearing Dakota lands from their rightful owners. Betrayed once again by broken treaties, the legal occupants would be forcibly transplanted from their homeland, or exterminated like pesky vermin.

Such a malevolent policy would be repeated over and over in the coming years until all Indians were imprisoned in miserable enclaves called "reservations"—or were dead.

Why did the leaders of this great, newly united country not publicly express their sympathies for our native Indians as they ostensibly had for the transplanted Africans?

Perhaps General Custer himself could answer this question for me should I be so fortunate as to meet him on my sojourn into the Black Hills.

In the main my trip to the Dakota Territory was uneventful, a succession of dreary inns, or miserable accommodations so primitive as to be undeserving of this appellation. I had not expected broad verandahs overlooking manicured gardens, but a succession of sod huts and ragged tents prompted me often as not to seek quiet solitude by my lone campfire.

Deadwood Gulch, my final destination, consisted of one long, narrow main street compressed between steep, timber-covered slopes on either side. Shabby tents and unpainted wooden false-fronted buildings lined the muddy thoroughfare, but from the cacophony of chopping, sawing, and hammering which echoed down the valley I knew Deadwood was a settlement roiling in the spasms of birth. All too soon these forested slopes would soon be denuded of their lush, verdant forests, their pristine beauty sacrificed for the construction of shabby dwellings and a potpourri of various establishments serving as rude monuments to man's lust for gold.

It came as no surprise that the most impressive, newly minted wooden buildings did not house schools or churches, but a succession of saloons, bordellos, or a combination of the two. A few hastily constructed and furnished hotels provided accommodations only marginally better than a cold campfire and bedroll.

Seemingly more care had been taken with the construction of lodging for animals than humans, for I easily secured eminently satisfactory arrangements for Corazón and my pack mule. Now it was time to begin mining the saloons.

Casually, over the next several weeks, I canvassed the numerous games of chance in the various establishments, neither winning nor losing amounts that would draw attention to me. It was soon obvious to one as experienced as I which gamblers were competent, who among them dealt crooked games, and which pokes were ripe for the picking.

I am not a man completely without conscience, and would rather, as much as possible, glean from the gamblers than the drones who had toiled long and hard for their slippery fortunes.

Poker is a game of skill and finesse. Cheaters are a despicable lot, whose dishonesty completely destroys the exhilarating intellectual exercise of probabilities, memory, and acting inherent in such games of chance. Dishonest scoundrels convert a fascinating challenge into a method of robbery, pure and simple. I could not abide such rascals, and generally avoided individuals and tables employing their nefarious schemes. Those who foolishly gamble without skill or intellect deserve to lose, but not to callous thieves.

My intense feelings on this subject unexpectedly shortened my stay in Deadwood, and opened the portal to a novel career. Once again, I would become a reluctant participant in yet another portentous event in American history.

Perhaps a lifetime of moderate affluence had quenched in me the fires of lust after wealth which consumed those unfortunates who deluged Deadwood in the vain hope of sudden riches. In less than a year, this sodden, cramped collection of dwellings had grown to a population of over 25,000 occupants. Every strata of society was represented, although the pool of citizens a man could trust with his poke or his life was exceedingly shallow.

In the endless games of chance which initially provided the settlement's only entertainment, I had learned early on to be a gracious loser when the occasion demanded, to win without bluster, and always to be seated with my back against the wall. Celebrating miners, freighters, and drifters of every conceivable stripe provided a steady source of revenue for the rapidly increasing cadre of professional gamblers. These sharks, in turn, supported my expenditures for comfortable lodging, good whiskey, and female companionship. As the town grew, these necessities exponentially increased in number, quality, and price.

Saloons, the sites of most of our poker games, rapidly effected the transition from comfortable to opulent, but their numbers were exceeded by the proliferation of houses of negotiable affection. In contrast to most of my confreres, I seldom visited these parlors of pleasure, satisfying my biological needs far more satisfactorily among the actresses from the troupes of players frequenting our opera house. Compared to the soiled doves, they were far more attractive, equally athletic, and far better conversationalists.

The long winter months of 1875 were thus passed rather pleasantly, particularly as the size and frequency of my bank deposits continued to increase. Deadwood to me was a bonanza. And I had not turned a spadeful of dirt.

Eagerly I awaited the coming of spring, for I found myself pondering more and more over the possibility of a visit with Mother at a site and climate pleasing to her. But the twists of fate once again enmeshed me in its coils.

Not infrequently we would be joined in our poker games by one or more Army officers temporarily residing in Deadwood to purchase supplies for their roving expeditions in the surrounding Black Hills. General Custer and his cohorts had discovered that their campaign to eliminate the Indian problem was far more effective when waged in the frigid winter months.

During that time, the roving Sioux warriors were concentrated in campgrounds with their women and children, thus far more vulnerable to attack. In such settlements they could be eliminated far more efficiently together with their ponies, teepees, and families. Those few who escaped such slaughter almost invariably starved or froze.

On rare occasions one of these visiting cavalry officers would be accompanied by an Indian scout employed by the troops, usually a Crow or half-breed. These scouts rarely joined the game, but sat silently observing yet another of the white man's foibles.

It began as a rather ordinary night. The dealer, who I had not seen before, was a thin, rather sallow individual with pomaded hair, drooping moustache, and a Derringer rather ostentatiously displayed in his left vest pocket. I distrusted him immediately. He was listlessly shuffling the cards as I assumed my usual chair seated to his left and introduced myself.

"Well, Mister Saint Helen," he responded in a high-pitched, almost effeminate voice, "I've been called many names, but Jack Slade will do for now. What's your pleasure?"

"An honest game and a few more players will do for now," I replied a little more harshly than I intended.

As if on cue, two men joined us. One, in the rather ill-fitting attire of a drover, said his name was Major Marcus Reno of General Custer's 7th Cavalry. He explained his shabby clothes by saying he did not enter saloons or gamble in uniform. His companion, obviously held in high regard by the major, was introduced as Mitch Bouyer, a part-Sioux scout, and, with obvious pride, Reno informed us that as a youth Bouyer had been trained by the legendary mountain man, Jim Bridger.

Chips were counted out and the game began. This night my cards were terrible, and I folded more hands than I played. Reno and Bouyer were winning frequent small pots while the larger ones almost always went to the dealer. It was an old gambler's ploy, and I watched Slade more closely. A few more hands made it apparent this gambler was out to fleece the half-breed, who he obviously disliked and spoke to with thinly disguised contempt.

In less than an hour I had discerned Slade was manipulating the cards, double-dealing and false shuffling. He was very adept at it, I must admit.

While the cards were being dealt for the next game of five-card stud, I spoke to Bouyer in Sioux: "Watch yourself, my friend, he is cheating you."

Major Reno seemed more surprised than Bouyer that I spoke the Sioux language, especially after the scout and I conversed further in this dialect.

Without a word of explanation, Bouyer suddenly announced in his heavily accented English: "Play no more. Me quit."

Slade was livid. "What the hell did you tell that Injun?" he spat at me.

I looked directly into the card shark's eyes and said slowly: "That you were cheating him."

His right hand snatched the Derringer from his pocket

and was halfway up his vest when my Prescott pointed at his lapel. I paused a split second for him to ponder his fatal mistake before my shot pierced the blackguard's hand and tore through his heart.

All the players and onlookers agreed I had acted in self-defense. There seemed to be no lawmen immediately available in Deadwood to investigate the incident, and, since I donated a sum for the disposal of Slade's body, the incident was closed.

Reno and Bouyer expressed no interest in continuing the game. It had been a bad card night for me, so I agreed to press on to another location for a nightcap.

During the ensuing conversation, Reno expressed considerable interest in my facility with the Sioux language, and to a lesser extent my use of the Prescott. After another round of drinks, he offered me a job as scout with the 7th Cavalry.

At first, the idea seemed so ludicrous I barely suppressed a chuckle. I, an unreconstructed Southerner with all my past activities, would be employed by bluebellies. But spring was in the air, the whiskey was excellent, and the episode with Slade suggested a temporary absence from Deadwood might be wise.

Two days later I was heading northwest with Reno's caravan to join General Custer's foray into Montana Territory. The illustrious general's mission would be to solve, as Major Reno put it, "the Indian problem in this part of the country for once and for all."

CHAPTER SEVENTEEN

Custer's winter campaign against the Sioux and Cheyennes had been an unmitigated disaster. The "peaceable" Indians had hunkered down on their assigned lands and caused no trouble, while the recalcitrant "hostiles" had easily escaped west to the rolling plains of Montana. The "Boy General" of such past renown, now only a lieutenant-colonel, seethed with frustration. He had been out-maneuvered and out-smarted by a people he regarded as subhuman, vastly inferior to all whites, and particularly to him. He vented his anger upon the officers and men of his command, scheduling endless drills and exercises, raging when these were not performed to his satisfaction. His rants often included threats of a firing squad for his hapless soldiers. This admonition was not an idle threat, for in his previous court-martial he had been found guilty of overzealous use of this ultimate mode of discipline.

Fortunately I had been assigned to the scouts under Major Reno, thus somewhat distanced from Custer's wrath. I would not have tolerated this fool's verbal abuse, thus bringing to an end both our careers,

Mitch Boyer and I became fast friends. From him and his fellow scouts I rapidly assimilated Indian language and lore, enhancing the knowledge imparted to me by Black Owl. Mitch was assigned directly to General Custer in recognition of his skills, and was intensely loyal to the man. Never would he allow derogatory remarks to be spoken of the general in his presence, and he followed his commander's orders without question, a trait that would be his undoing.

Most of the time White Swan, Major Reno's main scout, and I rode together as we ranged far ahead of the troops and wagons, often joined by Curley, a Crow who could ride like the wind. However, he spoke only a few words of English, and we communicated largely by sign language. Many of Custer's troops were European immigrants who also spoke only their native tongue, and I wondered how much confusion this would engender in crucial battlefield maneuvers.

It seemed to me that our force wandered rather aimlessly through the Black Hills as the weeks passed, and I suspect General Custer was searching more assiduously for gold than Indians. But eventually, as the weather became more pleasant, we traveled north to Fort Abraham Lincoln. I must admit an initial sense of unease and foreboding that fate had directed me to a fort with this appellation.

While the assembled troops busied themselves with the tedious process of refitting for the next campaign, commanders designed a strategy to crush the Sioux and Cheyenne tribes, forcing the survivors back onto the reservations.

Out of the south, from Wyoming, would come the army of General George Crook, including several hundred Crow and Shoshone Indians, sworn enemies of the Sioux. From the west marched a column led by Colonel John Gibbon. The troops of General Alfred Terry, including Custer's 7th Cavalry, would leave Fort Lincoln and travel southwest to join the others in a gigantic pincers movement to surround the Sioux and Cheyennes before they could disperse. Naturally it would be the task of each column's scouts to locate the Indian encampments.

With essentially no communication between the three columns, this plan seemed doomed to failure. Any substantial concentration of Indians could defeat or escape from one of the prongs, and to expect all three columns to co-ordinate a surprise attack on a large village before the inhabitants had escaped or effected a substantial resistance was ridiculous. These Cheyennes and Sioux were hardened, skilled warriors on their home ground fighting to protect their women and children, not cowed, semi-frozen non-combatants encountered by the bluecoats in past campaigns.

As we slowly moved west to our destiny, the other scouts and I reported, time after time, crossing wide trails left before the winter snows by ever-increasing numbers of Indians somewhere ahead of us. More ominously these trails extended from all angles of the eastern half of the compass, and appeared to lead to a common destination far over the western horizon.

None of the scouts had ever before encountered such a pattern. It was extremely rare for such a massive concentration of Indians to stay together for any length of time. Their enormous herds of ponies would graze the ground bare, while hunters must travel farther and farther from the encampment to find game.

As we progressed, the trails became increasingly fresh, but it was clear that the Indians ahead were moving leisurely across the plains, certainly not fleeing ahead of the troopers' advance. Custer smelled blood, and ordered a night march on the 24th of June, then halted in a deep divide just short of the Little Bighorn valley.

There was no sign of Crook's or Gibbon's forces, and we learned many days too late that Gibbon was still marching back and forth along the Yellowstone River awaiting word from General Terry.

171

One week before, of course unknown to us at the time, General Crook had fought a desperate battle with Crazy Horse and over 800 of his warriors far to the south. Crook had earned a Pyrrhic victory, but his losses necessitated a return to his base in Wyoming for regrouping.

As I recall the events of the next few days, I must conclude that General Custer would not have changed his course of action even if he had been aware that Crook and Gibbon would not be joining him for the crucial battle to come. I have never known such a war-lover, a man whose lust for battle was almost palpable. And whose total disregard for the safety of those under his command was reprehensible.

It was rumored that Custer considered himself to be a worthy candidate for the Presidency, and regarded his intended elimination of the "Indian problem" to be a giant steppingstone in that direction. The nation's first centennial would be celebrated less that two weeks hence, and I am certain that General Custer planned his conquering of the Sioux and Cheyennes as a spectacular present with appropriate fanfare and publicity from himself to the American voters.

On our trek from Dakota Territory I had very little direct contact with the general, who seemed to regard his scouts as necessary evils but only a step above his Indian adversaries. He was at least coldly cordial to my friend, Mitch Bouyer, on whom he relied to locate his enemies.

"Just lead me to them, Mister Bouyer . . . the Seventh and I will take care of the rest," we heard *ad nauseam*.

I never quite understood Mitch's allegiance to Custer, but he served the man with almost slavish devotion and followed his orders to the letter.

A detachment led by Major Reno was assigned the task

of exploring ahead of the main body of Custer's force. Mitch, another scout named Bloody Knife, and I ranged ahead of Reno's column. We promptly discovered the trail of an extremely large group of Indians headed in the direction of the Little Bighorn valley. Immediately upon hearing this news on the morning of June 22nd, Custer and the companies assigned to his direct command split off from General Terry's troops and gave chase. Terry had joined Gibbon's column to move down the Bighorn River, ultimately planning to rejoin Custer before any major engagement.

In his haste to overtake the Indians, Custer ordered a night march on the 24th while Mitch, I, and several other scouts climbed to an elevation on the divide that separated the Rosebud and Little Bighorn valleys. In the early mists of dawn we spotted the largest collection of Indians any one of us had ever seen. The settlement extended for at least three miles along the river. I estimated well over 10,000 occupants. Smoke from their teepees and campfires all but obliterated the horizon.

Mitch galloped back to the encampment and soon returned with Custer who insisted on confirming the news with his own eyes.

By the time Custer arrived, a dense morning haze permeating the river valley had obscured the view. Immediately it became patently obvious the general did not believe our report. I vividly recall Mitch pleading with him.

"General, on my word, there are more Indians down there than I have ever seen in one place. Thousands of them, and thousands of ponies. Our force is far too small."

"I will be the judge of that," Custer snapped, and mounted his horse. He snatched the reins to face us. "My men of the Seventh can defeat any number of hostiles. But they have marched all night and need rest. We will bivouac today and move into position at dawn." His eyes glowed with a feral gleam and his voice grew harsh. "Watch them. Watch them unceasingly. If any show the slightest sign of leaving, notify me immediately. None, none of these accursed redskins, I tell you, will escape."

He jerked his mount around savagely and galloped away before we could reply. Mitch and Bloody Knife remained on watch at the ridge while I rode back to advise Major Reno of Custer's strategy.

My briefing of the major had barely finished when Reno began pacing back and forth muttering to himself. Suddenly he exploded, exclaiming vehemently that it was blind folly to attack such an overwhelming number of Indians with our meager force of less than 700 men. Without doubt, he raged, we should await the arrival of Crook's and Gibbon's columns before any attempt was made to encircle the Indians and prevent their escape.

Reno planned to meet with Captain Benteen and other senior officers and attempt to dissuade Custer from attacking before reinforcements arrived.

They might have succeeded in convincing their impetuous commander, who knows? Fate often plays peculiar tricks, but none more grotesque than the loss of a few biscuits dooming Custer and his men.

General Custer returned to his sleeping troopers scattered about the campground to be greeted by his brother, Captain Tom Custer, with important news.

Tom was the true hero of the Custer family, having been awarded the Congressional Medal of Honor twice for incomparable bravery in the recent war.

Earlier that morning a small detail of Captain Custer's men had been sent back along the line of last night's march to recover a box of hardtack which had fallen from one of the supply wagons. They soon found the box—with several Indians sampling its contents. At the soldiers' approach, the startled warriors fled in the direction of their vast encampment.

To General Custer this could only mean that the Indian village would be warned of his soldiers' presence, and many would escape before the troopers could complete their encirclement.

All previous orders were cancelled. He would attack immediately.

This rash move was compounded by a series of unwise and ultimately fatal decisions. Custer had refused to utilize his newly issued rapid firing Gatling guns and left them behind, claiming they limited his mobility. For reasons known only to him, he would not incorporate units of Negro "buffalo soldiers" into his command, although they were considered by many to be the best Indian fighters in the Army. Custer tragically limited the effectiveness of his small force by splitting his troops into three separate units. Although he had shorn his distinctive shoulder-length blond hair, he insisted on wearing his striking, non-regulation hat into battle, thereby transforming himself into an alluring target for Indian sharpshooters. But no one argued with Custer without fear of rebuke or reprisals.

Captain Benteen with three companies of men was sent to the southwest to prevent the Indians' escape in that direction. I joined Major Reno and his three companies along the left bank of a small creek leading towards the Indian village, while Custer and five companies hurried along the right bank.

We had traveled about seven miles when a small group of Indians was spotted in the distance. They appeared to be fleeing, driving their cattle ahead of them. Custer ordered Major Reno and his companies to pursue the hostiles, while he would support us with his larger force should we encounter significant resistance.

A courier was dispatched to the pack train far to the rear of our position, ordering them forward. The supply wagons and their handlers included Custer's younger brother, Boston. Much later I learned that this impetuous youth, on hearing the news of the impeding battle, galloped forward to join his brother. His rash act would reap tragic and fatal consequences.

To Major Reno's everlasting credit, he did object vociferously to Custer's order. "Sir, I fear that splitting our meager force in the face of such overwhelming odds will prove disastrous. Should we not wait for reinforcements?"

Custer was furious. "You fear," he rasped, his voice tight. "I suspect that you fear too much, Major Reno. My troopers and I will be right behind you. Now get moving or go to the rear and I will find someone who can follow my orders."

Reno said nothing and clenched his teeth, his face dark with rage, and nudged his horse forward to rejoin his column.

I could remain silent no longer.

"General, you will be charging hardened Sioux warriors down there, not helpless women and children like you did on the Washita."

Custer was apoplectic. His hand moved to his holstered revolver. For a split second I prayed he would draw, but his hand dropped. He screamed at Reno's back.

"Major, take this . . . this half-breed with you. Put him in the very front of your charge. If he survives the day, a firing squad will deal with his damned impertinence later."

Reno and I galloped forward to his soldiers, and to the cataclysm that awaited us all.

Obeying the orders he knew to be flawed, Major Reno drew his cavalry into a line, bugles sounded, and we charged. Reno and I were in the front ranks and had not covered half the distance to the village when we spotted hordes of Indians racing down the slopes on both flanks, firing as they came. It was a trap, just as the major had suspected.

As I had tried to convince Custer, we were facing experienced, well-armed warriors, some equipped with repeating rifles. Reno masterfully marshaled his troopers into a defensive line and slowly retreated into a stand of timber, but had lost fully a third of his cavalry before we were able to regroup on a bluff above the river. Indians swarmed up the slope, their rifles spitting a withering fusillade.

And where was Custer? He was supposed to rush his column to our support when the battle commenced, but was nowhere in sight.

Captain Benteen had quickly realized his orders to surround the gigantic Indian village he encountered were ridiculous. He was returning with his men to join the main force when they heard the noise of our battle on the ridge and rushed to join us. The heroism of Benteen and his soldiers saved us all from certain annihilation, but the issue was still in doubt. We desperately needed Custer's five companies.

While the outnumbered soldiers lay behind the carcasses of their dead horses or dug shallow trenches to prepare for the next savage assault, Major Reno drew me aside.

"Your steed is much faster than any here. Take this note to Captain Tom Custer. The general might listen to him." He gripped my arm as I mounted Corazón. "Ride like hell,

Saint Helen. I do not know if we can hold them off till dark."

Corazón seemed to sense the urgency of our mission as we raced upstream along the ridges paralleling the river. About four miles from Major Reno lay the main ford of the Little Bighorn, surely to be Custer's crossing point.

I was wrong. He never reached the river. Just downstream from the ford on higher ground, Custer and his men were completely surrounded by a rapidly tightening noose of massed Indians firing, scalping, and mutilating the doomed troopers. I lay on the ridge top and observed the finale through my telescope. There was nothing I or anyone else could do to save Custer and his men now.

Many of the terrified troopers threw their weapons away, kneeled, and raised their hands in surrender, only to be shot or clubbed down without mercy. The remainder, realizing surrender was not an option, put revolvers to their temples and blew out their brains.

Custer was surrounded by a ragged circle of less than fifty soldiers, his clothes fouled with blood and grime. He was seated as if in a daze, the body of the eternally loyal Mitch Bouyer draped over his legs.

As the chaos of his folly swirled about him, Custer slowly raised his revolver and ended his life.

The egotistical stupidity of this accursed tyrant resulted in the slaughter of over 200 men, including Custer's two brothers and his brother-in-law, yet history records his name as a hero, and mine as a murderer.

The sane actions of Major Reno and Captain Benteen prevented the annihilation of troops under their command, yet they were vilified in the press as cowards. The Sioux and Cheyennes, defending their land and preventing the extermination of their women and children, were referred to as "bloodthirsty savages".

After Custer's self-imposed disaster, Indians of all tribes were pursued relentlessly by hordes of Federal troops and ultimately hounded into submission. Future historians will no doubt record many shameful sagas in the history of this nation, but none more disgraceful than the genocidal atrocities exacted upon its original inhabitants.

CHAPTER EIGHTEEN

By late afternoon I was able to rejoin Major Reno's embattled troopers without too much difficulty as the Indian attacks had begun to diminish. The next day we learned the sudden departure of many warriors was prompted by the sighting of General Terry's advancing column. During the night, women and children of the tribes magically dismantled their entire encampment and disappeared before sunup.

The entire débacle sickened me. Nothing had been gained by either side. No new territories, no riches or spoils of war, no noble causes to die for. The Sioux and Cheyennes had won a battle, but were doomed. All the fury of an enraged nation would be focused upon their certain submission or extinction. I had lost many dear friends, including Mitch Bouyer, for no good purpose.

No longer would I witness enforced obedience to insane commanders and its fatal consequences. After a brief farewell to Major Reno, I rode south alone.

Truly I had no particular destination in mind, and in retrospect the massacre had depressed me more than I realized at the time. Presumably either I or Corazón must have instinctively followed the tracks of our earlier journey into Montana, for I have little recollection of the route which brought us back to the outskirts of Deadwood.

With some effort, I can only remember a succession of dreary campfires on the stark, undulating prairie with little change of scenery until I reached the familiar Black Hills, now infested with gold seekers and the predators who followed in their wake like circling vultures.

During the few months since my departure, Deadwood had spread like a malignant growth upon the landscape. The town had grown much larger, but the bizarre architectural styles and shoddy construction continued unabated. Throughout the settlement there was an overwhelming sense of impermanence as if no one expected to live there, and the fragile buildings with their occupants could easily disappear overnight.

I first ensured a satisfactory berth for Corazón in one of the local livery stables, then established reasonably cozy accommodations for myself in the Gold Nugget Hotel. With ease and a great sense of relief, I discarded my rôle as half-breed tracker by means of a soaking hot bath, shave, haircut, and purchase of a totally new wardrobe. In less than a week after arriving, I had resumed the more comfortable persona of John St. Helen, gentleman gambler and *bon vivant*, worthy competitor in the innumerable and unceasing games of chance.

Once again the cards seemed to come my way, the gambling skills of *noveau riche* miners and other denizens of the gaming tables had not improved, and, as summer faded into autumn, my net worth steadily improved.

The joys of gaming were considerably improved by construction in early fall of the Bella Union Variety Theatre by Tom Miller, an entrepreneur from Cheyenne. Not only was every conceivable game of chance provided in opulent surroundings, first-class entertainment was presented on stage to enthusiastic audiences. Vaudeville acts, Shakespeare, dancing girls, and melodramas breathed new life into the often drunken and dreary events that had characterized post-sundown Deadwood. The arrival of comely actresses and dancing girls, I must admit, considerably altered my nocturnal activities and improved my general disposition. One of the more attractive attributes of these lovelies was their transient status, thereby avoiding entangling alliances, however pleasant.

Another of Miller's innovations, immediately successful, was the introduction of bare-knuckle prize fighting, with attendant frenzied wagering on the outcome. Personally I was almost sickened by the spectacle of two human beings caged in a ring, beating each other bloody or unconscious like trained beasts for the entertainment of a profoundly unsophisticated audience. However, I attended these functions occasionally only to wager on their outcome. As fate would have it, at one such event in the winter of 1876–1877 I met the man who would become one of my most venerable friends.

Two brawny weather-beaten pugilists were pounding each other unmercifully while a packed crowd of unkempt sadists roared their approval. This gentleman would have immediately garnered attention had he been attending an opera, but in this tempestuous gathering he stood out as if a spotlight shone upon him. Dressed entirely in black except for his starched white shirt, and thin to the point of emaciation, the handsome young man observed the combatants with as much interest as he would an insect on a windowpane. He was obviously a nocturnal creature, pale as bleached muslin, and he puffed lazily at a long black cheroot. He was new to this habit or tolerated it poorly, for his inhalations frequently precipitated spasms of racking coughs. Despite the stranger's frail appearance, there was a distinct aura of danger about the man. I immediately pegged him as a sophisticated gambler.

My initial impression was confirmed the following evening while I awaited a seat at his table as I noted the black-clad gentleman's dexterity with playing cards. We shook hands as I introduced myself and he responded: "John Henry Holliday, Mister Saint Helen. Just call me Doc. Everyone else does."

How could such a mellifluous voice resonate from such a wasted frame? His accent identified him as originating from Georgia or the Carolinas, and I suspected his measured bass tones bespoke a background in the theatre. Much later, when we had become fast friends, I learned I was only partially correct. Doc was reared in Georgia, but his only experiences in the theatre were as a member of the audience and, he laughingly admitted, rather close associations with a number of actresses.

As an infant, John Henry had undergone surgical repair of a cleft palate and had required extensive speech training as a child. Even as an adult I noted he avoided certain words and syllables, and spoke with a charming slowness and controlled timbre. Women, in particular, found his manner of speech irresistible.

His truly amazing skill at cards he attributed to his childhood companion, Sophie, a slave girl servant of his family who had taught young John Henry her innate ability to mentally calculate odds, percentages, and probabilities. He also laughingly associated his debilitating fondness to alcohol as originating with his being fed liquids from a shot glass for months prior to his oral surgery.

Doc's facility with knife and pistol were self-taught. Rumor had it these talents had been practiced not infrequently prior to his arrival in Deadwood.

John Henry's nickname was not misplaced, for he had come from a family tradition of physicians and dentists, and had graduated from a prestigious dental school in Philadelphia. He returned to his home in Georgia to practice his specialty, but developed consumption and moved to the sunshine and dry air of Dallas. His practice thrived, but he soon found his paroxysms of coughing unsettling to his patients. His ability as a dealer and gambler proved more lucrative than his dentistry, so he abandoned the latter and moved farther west. His itinerary carried him through Denver, Cheyenne, and on to Deadwood, leaving a trail of "incidents" in his wake. No doubt, his reputation for being equally adept with knife or gun preceded his arrival in Deadwood, for he was treated with unmistakable deference at the gambling tables. His legendary contempt for the lives of others paled in comparison with his own penchant for self-destruction. He ate sparingly if at all, avoided sobriety like the plague, and his nocturnal habits would exhaust the stamina of a hoot owl.

As the winter months dragged by, Doc and I became close friends, sharing a love for the Old South, now gone forever, good literature, and quiet genteel conversation. There was no better companion than Doc if he was sober, but I learned to excuse myself or avoid him when he had imbibed too much. At such times, regretfully all too frequent, he assumed the disposition of a constipated grizzly with hemorrhoids, and was twice as dangerous.

More than once I found it necessary quietly to disarm him and steer him to his lodgings to avoid tragic consequences. Later he always offered profuse apologies for his behavior and smothered me with expressions of appreciation. An exceedingly complex man, but I genuinely liked him. His choice of generally obsequious companions, however, left much to be desired.

One acquaintance of Doc's, who later became one of his closest friends, I disliked from our first meeting. Later, when I knew him better, I detested him. Maybe opposites do attract. In contrast to Doc's genteel manner, his new companion was rough in speech and appearance, seemingly always in a foul mood. When Doc introduced this person in his Southern drawl, I extended my hand and said: "Glad to meet you, White."

He ignored my proffered hand and growled: "My name is Wyatt, Wyatt Earp."

As if that name should mean something to me.

Earp was in town primarily to wager on the boxing matches, as one of his friends from Cheyenne, John Shannsey, was reputed to be a top contender, a "sure thing" according to Earp. Needless to say, Doc and I were encouraged to bet heavily on "Shanny". We did, and lost. Earp cried foul, but it was obvious his man was bested. I must say the loser did buy several rounds of consolation drinks for the three of us, and inadvertently during our conversation piqued my interest in a totally new line of work.

I had resolved to leave Deadwood in the spring and the warmer months were rapidly approaching. My plans were indefinite except to seek respite in warmer climes from gold seekers and their ilk. Earp regaled us at length with his plans to seek salaried employment as a lawman within Kansas or farther south. Silently I commiserated this was a wise move on his part, for he was an extremely inept gambler. I suspected his intention to become a lawman was based more on his desire to commit mayhem on his fellow human beings without fear of legal retribution, rather than any sense of civic duty.

In his ramblings Earp had unintentionally supplied me with an idea for future travel and employment. According to him, gunmen were being employed by railroads, stage lines, and freight companies to protect their cargoes and passengers from marauders by "whatever means deemed necessary".

Essentially these employees, disguised as ordinary travelers, were given a license to kill. In addition, vigilante groups and cattlemen's associations were surreptitiously hiring bounty hunters to seek out and "neutralize" perpetrators in areas devoid of effective law enforcement. Allegedly handsome salaries and bonuses were readily available for those who qualified.

His venture into the seamy profession of prize fighting having failed, Earp planned to resume family life and seek employment as town marshal in Dodge City. Doc also planned to move south, but his frail condition precluded extensive travel, and he regarded the great outdoors with as much relish as he would a tumble into a bed of cactus.

In the spring of 1877, the three of us boarded the Cheyenne and Black Hills stage with Corazón in tow, and headed for Cheyenne. From there we traveled much more comfortably via the Denver Pacific railroad to Denver. *En route,* Doc and I became even closer friends, enjoying innumerable games of poker and impromptu shooting contests from the rear of the train. Earp grudgingly joined us in the fun, but I never could get close to the man. He became much more contentious after I bested him with rifle and pistol while Doc lightened Wyatt's purse with cards.

In Denver I unloaded Corazón and said good bye to Doc and Earp. They would board the eastbound Kansas Pacific train, Doc going on to Kansas City to visit relatives while Earp would get off in mid-Kansas and head south to Dodge City. We all vowed to see each other again, but at the time I recall thinking this would be the last time I would see either of these gentlemen again.

CHAPTER NINETEEN

Since San Francisco I had not entered a city I enjoyed as much as Denver. All the luxuries and diverse pleasures of a large city were readily available, yet it still retained the bustle and enterprise of a growing small town.

And who could not appreciate its charming setting, with towering peaks to the west and rolling grassy prairie on the east. I easily obtained entirely satisfactory accommodations for Corazón and me, discovered establishments catering to a man's every need, and began to effect another change in character and appearance prior to seeking employment.

I luxuriated in the splendor of hot tub baths and obtained the services of an excellent barber and tailor. My suit coats were especially fashioned to conceal a supple new oiled leather holster and the indispensable Prescott.

John St. Helen, bachelor gentleman of expensive tastes, with an occult source of considerable wealth had emerged from his rather drab cocoon. Within a few weeks I had reached a surfeit of plays, operas, expensive dining, and attractive female companions. Flowers, gifts, and courtly manners never failed to open many bedroom doors.

In rented rigs and sometimes astride Corazón I had begun to enjoy riding alone in the nearby mountains. Sometimes I practiced my skills with rifle and pistol, but most often I left the city to experience the joys of solitude, and the panoramic vistas of pristine beauty in the valleys below.

For some peculiar reason I was often drawn to Prospect Point, a site not appreciably different from other lovely spots, but alone on this high escarpment I experienced an inner current of tranquility, almost bliss, that for a few fleeting moments suggested that even I might have a soul.

But I could control my restless spirit no longer, despite the pleasures of my idle life in Denver. It seemed prudent to consolidate all my sources of income from the trust fund in a Canadian bank, my investments, and my Dutch benefactor into one local establishment.

Cattlemen's, one of the largest banks in Colorado, had been highly recommended. When I chanced upon their newspaper advertisement for men "of sterling character and impeccable aim" to protect their shipments, it seemed to be ordained that I should become a customer and employee of this firm.

Interviews pursuant to my deposits and withdrawals proceeded graciously at Cattlemen's. Application for employment required a little more effort. Initially I was escorted into a rather cramped office and seated before an obese, florid-faced walrus whose name plate on his tiny desk identified him as **Frederick Tweed, Ass't. V.P.** He studiously ignored me for what seemed to be an eternity while pretending to study a sheaf of papers through his miniscule pince-nez spectacles. Without a word of introduction he retrieved a printed form from his desk drawer and began to quiz me concerning name, date of birth, *et cetera*. Not once did he look up at me from his paper. I do not suffer fools easily, and cannot abide bad manners or rudeness. He reached to dip his pen in the inkwell while inquiring: "Any proficiency with firearms?"

Before his nib reached the ink, the barrel of my Prescott obstructed his left nostril.

"That is speed," I whispered. "Shall I now demonstrate accuracy?"

Tweed gulped twice, unable to speak.

"Perhaps I should conclude this interview with a more senior member of the firm," I offered, and holstered my weapon.

Tweed remained speechless, but nodded and bolted from the office, almost tripping in his haste. He did not return.

Less than a minute passed. A prim matronly female with thick glasses and graying hair pulled tightly in a bun appeared and suggested politely that I might accompany her to the office of Mr. Christian Gaylord, president of Cattlemen's Bank.

Mr. Gaylord's office was not small. Several overstuffed chairs covered in leather, a massive desk, walls of bookcases, and a lavishly stocked bar that would do justice to the finest saloon did not crowd the room. The appearance of the man before me put to rest all my previous conceptions of bank presidents. His immaculately tailored suit emphasized his trim athletic physique, his black mane was barely streaked with gray, and my attention was immediately drawn to his penetrating ice-blue eyes, the eyes of a gunman.

Introductions were exchanged, we sat, and Mr. Gaylord smiled.

"Mister Saint Helen, I am not accustomed to interviewing armed men in this office, as you might imagine. Therefore, we could proceed much more comfortably if you would place any weapons in your possession on my desk."

Of course I immediately did as he requested. His wry smile reappeared.

"Now both of us can breathe easier. I must tell you the only exit to this office is securely locked, two marksmen are concealed behind the bookcases, and you do not appear to be a man who would want to die today. Shall we press on with the interview?"

I returned his smile and nodded my assent. I liked this man.

Without a surplus word or phrase, Gaylord detailed his concept of the position and the type of man he was looking for to fill it. Cattlemen's Bank shipped and received large amounts of money by stage, rail, and private messenger throughout the Southwest. Law enforcement in this vast area was spotty, unreliable, and to a large extent non-existent. Therefore, the time and amount of such shipments were known only to selected senior officers of the bank.

In addition, strongboxes containing nothing but sand were occasionally transported under the usual heavy security in a further effort to confuse potential bandits. Armed guards disguised as ordinary passengers accompanied all shipments, sham or real. These men were instructed to kill, without mercy, anyone who attempted to steal their cargo.

"As you might imagine, Mister Saint Helen, it is difficult to hire qualified men willing to risk their lives possibly defending a box of dirt. The pay is excellent, but it is not a life for a married man . . . or one with obligations. Interested?"

I nodded without speaking.

"Very well, then. I can see by the Prescott, you are an excellent judge of weapons, and from Mister Tweed's breathless testimony I learned you possess a lightning-quick draw. Any additional qualifications you would care to mention?"

It was no time to be modest.

"Mister Gaylord, sir, I am single and presently . . . unattached. I am an excellent marksman with rifle or pistol, and have been employed previously in similar positions to the one you described. I can track an eagle to its nest, a panther to its lair, or an outlaw to his hide-out. I speak English, Spanish, and the Sioux dialect. In less than an hour I could change my clothing, speech, and mannerisms so you would not recognize me on my return. Chameleon-like, I can meld with any strata of society including sophisticates, Indians, Mexican bandits, and soldiers. You will find me to be a faithful, honest, and reliable employee. The salary is of minor importance except for expenses . . . ridding society of its scurrilous vermin is payment enough.

"Let me make my personal philosophy abundantly clear. I kill not for pleasure or money, but because there are persons who I feel need to be absented from this earth, and I am the instrument for their removal.

"However, I respectfully request that you do not ask and I will not answer any questions about my background. You have my word as a gentleman that to my knowledge I am not wanted by the law."

Gaylord tilted the leather chair back and laced his fingers behind his head. "Just one more question, Mister Saint Helen, if I may. When can you start?"

It was my turn to smile. "Tomorrow, sir, would be fine."

We rose and shook hands. "Excuse my presumption, Mister Gaylord, but your eyes. I have only seen such coloration in men very adept with weapons . . . on both sides of the law."

Gaylord's wide grin split his face. I am certain I heard a muffled chuckle from one of the concealed bodyguards.

"You flatter me, sir. Yes, as a youth I was considered quite a marksman. But fortunately I learned a valuable lesson early in life. Far more money could be garnered managing and owning banks than robbing them." He hefted my Prescott admiringly, then returned it to me. "My representative will come to your hotel this evening with detailed confidential instructions, Mister Saint Helen. Good luck . . . and good hunting."

CHAPTER TWENTY

Two days after my interview with Mr. Gaylord I was jostling with my fellow passengers in a stagecoach headed south for Santa Fé. My recent journey to Denver, primarily by rail, must have spoiled me, for the discomforts of this trip became almost unbearable long before we reached our destination. The legendary charm of Santa Fé completely evaded me. I am not an admirer of Spanish architecture or customs, and find no pleasure in perpetually blowing dust.

The return journey was equally uneventful, but each turn of the squeaking coach wheel brought us closer to Denver and the cool mountain air.

A short, albeit very enjoyable, week's respite was spent taking Corazón out for runs, sighting in a more powerful telescope for my Winchester, and nocturnal assignations of a most pleasurable kind.

My next assignment was scheduled to be a fast round trip by rail to Cheyenne. There would be no passengers, only the locomotive, mail car, and caboose. No stops except to replenish fuel and water for the engine. One guard would ride with the engineer, one in the mail car, and I would guard the rear from the caboose. We left Denver in the dead of night, and from the large number of armed personnel present at our departure I suspected, this trip, our strongboxes and safes did not contain sand.

No one slept that night, but morning found us safely in Cheyenne. While we downed a hasty breakfast served at our posts, the cargo was unloaded into wagons surrounded by hard-eyed men cradling carbines or shotguns. New trunks and safes were trundled into the boxcar, doors were locked, and we began our return to Denver without so much as a toot on the whistle.

A little more than halfway home, as we were slowed by a slight incline, they were waiting. The gentle curve of the tracks allowed me to see from the window of the caboose a pile of logs obstructing the track ahead. While the engineer slowed to a stop, I climbed on the roof of the caboose with my Winchester and a full box of cartridges. I lay flat, concealed from view, and scanned the wooded promontory overlooking the roadblock with my telescopic sight. I saw no one.

It was deathly quiet except for the hiss of escaping steam from the halted locomotive. This eerie calm was shattered by a yell from the wooded knoll just ahead of our train.

"Unlock them damned boxcar doors and shove out the safes. Else we'll blow y'all to hell."

"Come and get it, you bastards!" was heard from the boxcar.

"We got dynamite up here, damn your soul!" the bandit roared.

"Bring it on!" said the boxcar.

Now I glimpsed movement on the ridge, less than 100 yards from me. I sighted through the scope, a head popped up into the crosshairs, and I blew it to pulp.

It was like a shooting gallery. A robber's head would appear as he threw the dynamite, I splattered his brains with a well-aimed shot, and his missile exploded ineffectually on the side of the hill. Another fool would try the same maneuver. These men were dumber than dirt. Not one of them could have thrown the sticks from the ridge far enough to damage us, but they never learned.

I shot the fourth man before he could release his stick with its sputtering fuse. A gout of débris mixed with body parts erupted from behind the ridge and the battle ended.

We did not tarry to investigate the remote possibility of any survivors. Nevertheless, I remained on guard from the caboose roof while our crew cleared the tracks, then we thundered on safely into Denver.

Less than a week after this episode, I was summoned by messenger to Mr. Gaylord's office. His receptionist greeted me as warmly as she would have a spitting cobra. Like a teacher correcting an errant pupil, she informed me that Mr. Gaylord instructed her to secure my weapon in the lock box on her desk. She pronounced "weapon" as if the syllables rasped her tongue.

I complied with her request and was ushered into his lavish sanctum. Gaylord's steely eyes flashed as he complimented me on my handling of the recent episode on the Cheyenne run. After we were seated and cigars were lit, he first assured me no one was hidden behind his bookcases.

"What I have to say to you now, Mister Saint John, is in the strictest confidence and for our ears only, agreed?"

I nodded, exhaling a wreath of aromatic smoke from a truly fine cigar.

"Do you have any objections to traveling, and particularly working alone?"

"None in the least, sir. In fact, I prefer it."

"Good," Gaylord replied, obviously pleased. "I thought so. Now let me give you a little background information leading up to what I trust will be an association of mutual benefit."

As if lecturing to an enraptured audience, Gaylord eloquently expounded his encyclopedic knowledge of past and current events which had shaped the West and his vision for the future.

The era of an open range was drawing to a close, strangled by the recent invention of barbed wire. No longer would cattle graze freely until rounded up and driven to market. Smaller, fenced ranches containing branded cattle with improved breeding would forever change the quality and price of beef. These animals would be tempting targets for the army of rustlers who could now realize far greater profits from fewer stolen cattle. No longer would these thieves find it necessary to conduct massive raids into Mexico for the rangy longhorns and hope to dispose of their herd before capture or discovery on the slow trek north. The smaller ranches could not afford to hire enough gunmen to protect their expensive beeves from the predatory rustlers, and were at their mercy.

"Most banks, in particular this one, have invested heavily in the cattle business," Mr. Gaylord said, and leaned forward over his desk, his blue eyes alight. "And I mean to protect my investments. These rustlers have become more than a damn' nuisance. Their numbers are growing, they are well armed and led, and ruthless to a man. Our bank, with many others in this area, have for some time employed the Pinkertons. You have heard of them, I presume?"

I nodded, anxious for Gaylord to continue his oration.

"The Pinkertons have operatives who have infiltrated most of the larger bands of rustlers and have learned who their leaders are and who finances them. But the dirty work is left to the hirelings and it would be well nigh impossible to prosecute their leaders in a court of law. Evidence of their involvement is difficult to prove, and unfortunately many lawmen and judges are in their pocket."

Mr. Gaylord rose from his chair and began pacing, puffing his cigar mightily.

"The best way to kill a snake is to cut off his head. What I need is a man who can rid this country of some snakes. Are you that man?"

I nodded again.

CHAPTER TWENTY-ONE

For nearly two years I roamed the West, through Colorado, Wyoming, Montana, New Mexico, and northern Arizona, leaving behind a series of what I would prefer to call executions. My trust in Gaylord was absolute, for we never communicated directly at any time. My instructions would arrive by mail or telegram and I burned the contents after reading them. Travel was generally by rail or horseback, as I avoided uncomfortable stagecoaches as much as possible. Sometimes Corazón would accompany me in a boxcar and I would ride him to a destination, but most often I rented mounts, changing them as often as I changed disguises.

Usually I enjoyed a welcome respite of a month or more between assignments, and always spent this time in Denver. Books, leisurely walks, and riding Corazón into the nearby mountains occupied my days, while at night good food, good companions, and various cultural pursuits eliminated any trace of *ennui*.

Without realizing it, I had markedly reduced my intake of alcohol during these years, even during my "vacations" in Denver. The appeal of gambling had lost some of its luster and I tended to find companions, male and female, in good restaurants, plays, and occasional operas. Possibly the intense concentration and constant alertness which my work required subconsciously stimulated my instinct for self-preservation, and diminished the appeal of activities which dulled my responsiveness.

And, too, aside from the absolute necessity for mental

fitness in my rôle as a hired exterminator, physical salubrity was mandatory. The rigors of long journeys, the absolute necessity for secrecy and stealth, and the obligatory "keen eye and a steady hand" at the inevitable dénouement required me to maintain the most exemplary health of my career.

Mr. Gaylord had been indubitably correct in his summation at our first meeting. In my travels I had figuratively removed many heads, and many snakes had died. Large scale rustling in Colorado was a thing of the past, and almost non-existent in adjacent states or territories. But the incidence of stagecoach and train robberies was rapidly increasing, particularly in the lawless regions far to the southwest of Denver.

Large deposits of silver had been discovered in Arizona Territory close to the Mexican border. Shipments of this precious metal were of necessity transported for considerable distances by vulnerable stagecoaches to the nearest railhead, and bandits pounced like vultures. Pursuit by pathetically inefficient lawmen was desultory and ineffective. Often the robbers would disappear into Mexico, immune from capture.

According to Mr. Gaylord, Cattlemen's Bank possessed several significant financial interests in these silver mines and their product. He wished to insure these investments were sound. It was time to behead more snakes.

In early autumn of 1880, I wended my way to the miserable hamlet of Tombstone, Arizona. Even Deadwood could not rival this burg in its unpleasant climate, ramshackle appearance, and number of miscreants. Few residents were gainfully employed. Most of the population seemed to be involved in gambling, prostitution, or chronic drunkenness.

The hapless miners, many imported from Mexico, toiled

endlessly for meager wages that they promptly squandered in the fleshpots of Tombstone. Their shafts tunneled extensively under the town and I pondered the poetic justice of a collapse of the entire city into a hell created from their own greed.

Adding considerably to my distaste was the presence of the infamous Wyatt Earp and his sorry brothers. The Earps were involved in a number of businesses in town, including mines, saloons, and probably brothels. Somehow Wyatt's brothers were involved in law enforcement, so I heard, but I never took time to learn the details. I avoided the whole clan as much as possible. Wyatt never recognized me in my rôle of a businessman from Colorado surveying silver mines as possible investment opportunities.

Soon after arrival, I concluded a portion of the assignment for which I had been dispatched. Apparently such happenings were of little interest or more commonplace around this area than I had expected, for the accomplishment thereof rated only two paragraphs in the Tombstone newspaper. More verbiage was devoted to the drunken antics of one John Ringo. This locally notorious lout had fallen from his horse into the watering trough fronting the Oriental Saloon. From there he screamed obscenities at passers-by until quieted by a rap on the head with a revolver wielded by his erstwhile companion, one Wyatt Earp.

I had encountered this Ringo in a local restaurant soon after arrival in Tombstone. He had staggered against my table upsetting my coffee into my food and stumbled out the door without a word of apology. Only my need to maintain a low profile because of my mission prevented me from ending his boorish life at that instant.

Attention to business required my absence from Tombstone for a short time, and upon successful completion of negotiations, so to speak, I returned to a reunion with one of my true friends, John Henry Holliday.

While I was breakfasting in the hotel's restaurant, Doc shambled in, obviously intoxicated at that early hour. He flopped into a chair, ordered black coffee, and immediately was doubled over by racking, productive coughs. Doc looked like death warmed over. He had lost weight, his clothes were untidy, and his distinctive voice was a garbled croak. Pity forced me to join him.

When I introduced myself, he gazed at me for a moment in disbelief, then focused his eyes with difficulty and stood up unsteadily to envelop me in his arms. It was as if he were a drowning man clutching his last hope.

In spite of his protestations, I insisted he eat a hearty breakfast and down copious drafts of coffee. In reply to his questions, I continued my rôle as a successful businessman and potential investor. Doc's life had plummeted downhill like a runaway cart since Deadwood. He had almost completely abandoned the practice of dentistry and had been involved in several shooting scrapes since we had last met. While in Dodge City he had somehow saved Wyatt Earp from an early demise, and they had become fast friends. Doc had come to Tombstone from Prescott to join Earp in some of his enterprises, but his long-time love, one Mary Katherine Harmony, had refused to come with him primarily because of her dislike and distrust of the Earps. Kate, as Doc called her, had traveled to Globe, Arizona, where Doc feared she had "gone into business for herself." This break-up had precipitated Doc's most recent spree.

I postponed my plans for the next couple of weeks and nursed Doc back to a semblance of health. Rest, sunshine, an adequate diet coupled with a temporary abandonment of his suicidal life style worked wonders. His resiliency astounded me.

While involved in Doc's rehabilitation, I seized the opportunity to invest some personal funds in the burgeoning silver mines. This venture was significantly enhanced by the telegraphed advice of Mr. Gaylord, and ultimately proved quite lucrative

Doc promised me faithfully he would take better care of himself and even toyed with the idea of setting up a dental office. When I left, he was anticipating a possible reunion with his beloved Kate who he had bombarded with plaintive letters.

I completed another "piece of business" without incident, said farewell to a rejuvenated (at least for the time being) Doc Holliday, and returned to Denver.

CHAPTER TWENTY-TWO

"Good news, Pres." Ken turned from his word processor as I entered his study. "I got an e-mail from my buddies in Washington yesterday, and they verified the paper in Booth's journal is late Eighteen Hundred's vintage. And get this, the handwriting matches Booth's diary in their archives . . . at least close enough that they're willing to say the diary and the journal were probably written by the same person. I'm no lawyer, but this looks like pretty firm evidence that Booth lived and kept his memoirs."

"You bet," I answered less enthusiastically than Ken expected. "But my news isn't so great. Some of the pages are practically illegible, and a few are missing."

"Very many?"

"There doesn't seem to be. As I copied the journal, I've taken the liberty of filling in illegible words with what I think Booth would have written, but the pages aren't numbered so I don't know if they've been removed, or he just didn't make a journal entry."

Ken smiled wryly. "It seems there's lots we'll never know about Booth. Unfortunately I've also learned the mummy's DNA isn't much help. It doesn't match any in the agency's criminal files, but they'd need a specimen from a close relative of Booth's to say whether the mummy is or isn't our man."

"That's probably another blind alley," I said dejectedly, and flopped into Ken's recliner. "With all his philandering, God knows how many women he gave syphilis while he was in the infectious stage. But, of course, they didn't know the etiology of this disease until early in the Nineteen Hundreds. I'm sure Wilkes has numerous illegitimate descendants, but the guy was such a chameleon they never knew or cared who their ancestor was. I've found several accounts alleging Booth's secret marriage to an Isola D'Arcy, and a son and daughter born to this union, plus references to a couple of other probably fictional marriages. But even if they exist, I doubt if we could locate anyone who'd want to be identified as a descendent of John Wilkes Booth. And just five years ago, a court in Maryland dismissed a formal request to exhume the supposed body of Booth from the cemetery in Baltimore for 'insufficient evidence'. So that route is closed, too."

"Well, Pres, don't give up yet. Although"—Ken turned back to his console—"I told you writing fiction would be a lot easier."

BOOK FOUR

Stop it at the start,
it's late for medicine to be prepared,
when disease has grown strong through long delays.

Remedia Amoris
Ovid

CHAPTER TWENTY-THREE

John Ringo should never have shot my horse. I would have most assuredly killed the drunken lout as I promised Doc, but Ringo's demise undeniably would have been less prolonged and significantly less unpleasant had he not nettled me so.

I had no animosity toward the man. I knew him only casually, and found no reason to expand our relationship. During my mercifully brief term of residence in Tombstone some years earlier, I had scrupulously avoided any association with individuals or factions involved in the numerous shoot-outs which made this dreary mining town famous. These amateurish confrontations accomplished nothing except to furnish ample fodder for newspapers and a form of biologic natural selection for the area's inhabitants.

Killing Ringo was simply a matter of performing a favor for my friend. As Doc would put it: "A friend will help you . . . a good friend will help you hide the body."

I had enjoyed Doc Holliday's company from the moment I met him in Deadwood, and this relationship ripened even more during our brief association in Arizona, for he seemed to be one of the few educated men in Tombstone. His placid Southern accent provided blessed relief from the mangled, ungrammatical Spanish-English cacophony spouted by most of the locals. With Holliday I could slake my thirst for some reasonably sophisticated discourse on subjects other than cattle, whiskey, and whores. It was he who had convinced me that silver mines in Leadville, Colorado would be far wiser investments than the depleting resources surrounding this rude excuse for an Arizona town prophetically named Tombstone. The long days I spent in that locality were endurable only because they proved so lucrative in terms of investments and the wealth of interesting characters gravitating there like moths unto a candle. Many who visited this pathetic settlement found permanent repose after venturing too close to the flames of greed, mendacity, and deceit that flickered perpetually in that den of vipers.

Doc maintained that Tombstone provided a hot, arid climate beneficial to his smoldering consumption. If so, this benefit was far outweighed by his unending indulgence in bad whiskey, fondness for loose women, and a predilection for choosing dangerous companions. I had no doubt that such involvement would result in his early demise, but I truly believe he subconsciously sought this manner of sudden death rather than slowly coughing up his lungs, piece by bloody piece.

Certainly his affiliation with the infamous Earp clan could bring him nothing but grief, and I never understood his fascination with this dysfunctional family and their escapades other than an unrealized death wish.

Wyatt, the titular leader of this sorry bunch, possessed an exaggerated sense of his own importance and sported his firearms with more bravado than skill. He and his brothers traveled together like a pack of jackals, a practice no doubt necessary for their survival.

I was more than pleased and greatly relieved when Doc left Tombstone in the spring of 1882 and joined me in Leadville, a much healthier environment for both of us, despite the thin air and long winters. But Doc's journey was not entirely voluntary. He had been arrested on a charge of larceny and transported to Pueblo, then released on bail pending a grand jury investigation. Straightaway he visited me in Leadville to request my services in eliminating the source of his discontent, one John Ringo. This swaggering bully, cut from the same cloth as the Earps, had vexed me on occasion during my long months in Arizona, so no persuasion was required for me to remedy this unpleasant business, *pro bono,* of course.

In June, I saddled old reliable Corazón once more and left the cool Colorado mountains for the familiar wastelands of southern Arizona to ply my trade. While riding, I reflected that 1882 was almost half over, and for the first year in many I had not killed anyone. Perhaps I had been too intent on substantially increasing my net worth through sage investments in the mining of silver. This failing would soon be remedied.

John Ringo's path could have been followed by a harelipped bloodhound. For the first week in July, he toured one saloon after another in Tombstone, then departed for nearby Galeyville, leaving behind irate proprietors clutching unpaid bar bills.

In the sterile, unforgiving desert country just north of Galeyville, I spotted him. Although it was not yet noon, the sun was blistering. Shimmering heat waves blurred his image. The fool was hatless, swaying drunkenly, both hands gripping the saddle horn. Certainly the sun and the alcohol would have finished him by evening, but I would not be denied.

Perhaps the heat had dulled my senses or my vision was distorted, for Ringo abruptly turned and fired before I could react, then tumbled from his saddle and lay immobile on the rocky ground.

In a heartbeat I was standing over him, pistol in hand. He had not moved, but snored like the drunken pig he was while foul spittle dried on his fissured lips.

A horrible sound behind me whirled me about, crouched, revolver in hand. It was Corazón—spraddle-legged, wheezing ominously, bloody foam spewing from his nostrils. Ringo's bullet had pierced the poor beast's lungs. There was nothing I could do.

Averting my head, I ended Corazón's agony with a single shot. Ringo would not die so easily.

I removed my saddle from the dead animal and cringed at the thought of leaving him for the buzzards, but a fire might attract unwelcome guests and divert me from my plans for Ringo. White-hot anger supplanted my grief as I turned my attention to Corazón's killer.

First, I scalped him. Not completely, just a sample along his forehead, but quite adequate to awaken fully the desperado. His bleary eyes widened in horror as I described in graphic detail some of the quaint procedures reserved for thieves and horse killers I had learned from *Don* Melitón's Apache trackers years ago.

With a little encouragement from my Colt, he removed his boots and tossed them away. I graciously allowed him to staunch the dripping scalp wound with a dirty bandanna, then had him shoulder my heavy saddle and walk ahead of me after I mounted his horse.

We were barely a mile from my destination in a cottonwood grove ahead, but the rocks and cactus had razored his feet into a bloody mess before we were halfway there. With my generous permission, he wrapped the tatters of his hose and filthy undershirt over his feet and tottered on, cursing bitterly with each step. He should have been grateful I allowed him to wear his hat, but this kindness was not from any concern on my part for his welfare, but the constant buzzing of large green flies around his gaping scalp wound annoyed me.

In the clump of trees I bade him sit with his back propped against a trunk while I reprised for him my knowledge of interesting Apache customs.

A victim without hope soon becomes altogether too compliant and thereby uninteresting, so I offered Mr. Ringo a challenging proposal. I would load his revolver with one cartridge and allow him to blow out his own brains, or I could commence a rather painful and prolonged vivisection, beginning with his private parts.

My descriptive powers exceeded my expectations, for he immediately chose the quick demise and executed this option with perfection.

A perverse notion to confuse anyone who might discover Ringo's body before the varmints and buzzards had finished their work compelled me to reload his pistol except for the spent cartridge and replace it in his right hand. I leaned his rifle against the tree trunk and buckled his spare cartridge belt upside down above the other to muddy the waters of deduction further. Would the investigator's verdict be murder or suicide?

I tied my saddle behind Ringo's, mounted his horse, and rode leisurely to the nearest stage stop. Retrieving my possessions, I spooked his horse to gallop away and rested on my saddle until the coach arrived.

Over far too many years I had traveled the West, and occasionally beyond, ridding our environment of vermin who needed killing. At times my services were for hire, often I acted of my own volition. Never, to the best of my knowledge, was anyone eliminated whose absence did not significantly benefit society. And of all the ones I "absented", no death gave me greater personal satisfaction than John Ringo's.

I really loved that horse.

CHAPTER TWENTY-FOUR

The town of Leadville was renowned more for its storybook characters than the legendary bounty from its innumerable mines. Meyer Guggenheim, Soapy Smith, Maggie Brown, the Tabors, Broken Nose Scotty, Susan B. Anthony, and Chicken Bill Lovell all paled in comparison with an individual who had arrived in our fair city while I was in Arizona.

Oscar Wilde, an English gentleman some fifteen years younger than I, was lecturing throughout the country following his eminently successful play, *Vera, or The Nihilists*, produced in New York City. Apparently he had been enticed to visit Leadville by a truly impressive sum solicited from various wealthy pseudo-intellectuals of our city. These pretentious souls labored under the assumption that sophistication and culture could be purchased like women and real estate.

I would have expected that Oscar's appearance alone would have immediately effected hoots of derision if not painful verbal and physical abuse from the uncouth denizens of our provincial settlement. His lofty frame was topped by shoulder-length hair, and he was clothed in velvet knee breeches, gaudy sashes, and silk cravats. In voice and mannerisms he reminded me most vividly of my brother Joseph, still an unpleasant recollection after all these years. To portray dear Oscar as the antithesis of Leadville's rough-hewn, rugged miners and teamsters would be a monumental understatement. But from the moment he appeared on stage and began his lecture, these illiterate bumpkins were mesmerized. By the time I had returned from my business trip to Arizona, Oscar was lionized to the point of worship and was the toast of the town.

When I was finally able to press through the sycophantic mob that surrounded him even at meals and introduce myself, I shall never forget his reply.

He smiled seductively, batted his long lashes, and cooed: "Oooh, Saint Helen. That would be a more appropriate name for me, don't you think?"

It was the beginning of a beautiful friendship.

Not since Francisca had I found someone who could discuss Shakespeare with such intellectual probity, and his keen knowledge of other English classics compared favorably with my own. Our eclectic tastes were remarkably similar, extending from an abiding love of great literature to the reckless imbibing of strong drink and fascination with games of chance. The only facet of our characters we did not share was my abiding appreciation of the opposite sex.

I once commented on our mutual indulgence in practices many would consider self-destructive, a remark which caused him to ponder a moment, then reply: "You know, John, you are right. Each man often kills the thing he loves, and I most certainly love myself, don't you?"

We laughed heartily at the time, but in retrospect Oscar had perfectly summarized my personality, and probably his, also.

All good things, unfortunately, must come to an end, and so it was with Oscar's stay in Leadville. News of his imminent departure spread like an ominous thundercloud over the populace. The miners became more distressed than the self-serving intelligentsia who had invited him and began immediate preparations for a unique farewell banquet in his honor.

Deep in the recesses of the vast Wolfstone Mine, these toilers converted their underground lunchroom into a lavishly decorated saloon and prepared an opulent feast to honor their hero. After everyone was satiated with food and drink, Oscar rose to deliver his farewell remarks. The overpowering din ceased so suddenly and completely that for a moment I feared I had become deaf.

Beginning with—"My beloved troglodytes . . . ,"—Oscar delivered a brief oration of such magnificence and poignancy that the entire assembly of the most hard-nosed men on earth was moved to racking sobs and tears. I must confess my eyes, too, were wet.

At the end he challenged them all to try and drink him under the table. The answering roar was of such volume that I feared the very walls of our cavern would rupture. After several hours Oscar had gained yet another triumph despite the miners' gallant efforts. Many did not report to work for several days thereafter.

Next morning, chipper as ever and none the worse for wear, Oscar embraced me, then departed on the eastbound coach, waving his kerchief gaily in farewell until he disappeared over the hill. I have not seen him since.

I realize now that the time in Leadville represented an undetected watershed in my life, for soon after I began to experience an almost imperceptible decline in my usually excellent health.

CHAPTER TWENTY-FIVE

The onset of my malady was so insidious that, for some time, I did not recognize the symptoms, usually dismissing them as lingering effects of the previous night's festivities. But soon after Oscar's departure, I first noted a slight diminution in accuracy during target practice. This was not consistent, and I initially attributed the problem to substandard ammunition. But I also realized, while reading, that my visual acuity had declined although certainly not sufficiently for me to consider corrective lenses. After all, I reasoned, I was no longer a young man, but refused to think of myself as old. The increasing irritability and occasional insomnia I dismissed as the return of vagabond impulses that had tormented me all my life.

In an idle moment I speculated on the possibility I had contracted some unknown infectious illness from the infamous blanket episode during my service in the Confederate conspiracy. My colleagues and I had purchased several trunks of blankets used by British troops in Bermuda during an outbreak of smallpox and yellow fever and had these infected items distributed throughout Washington with only marginal success. My exposure had been minimal, but medical knowledge of such diseases remains miniscule.

Probably some months later I began to notice subtle changes in balance coupled with a slight change in gait as if my feet sometimes did not know where they were. Again, I paid little attention to such symptoms at the time, only recalling these early signs when my condition worsened.

Much more distressing to me was a marked decline in my tolerance for alcohol. This soon reached the point that I became a very fastidious drinker, much to the dismay and derision of my constantly imbibing confrere, Doc Holliday. Much less disturbing to Doc was the significant deterioration of my legendary skill at cards. For a time he profited substantially until I realized my celebrated memory for cards played and mental calculations of probabilities was almost non-existent. Henceforth I folded at the slightest provocation, evoking howls of anguish from Doc as he witnessed the sudden demise of his golden goose.

In a rash moment I queried Doc concerning my symptoms and was dismissed with: "Hell, John, come see me if you've got a bad tooth. Go see a real doctor if anything else is bothering you."

I took his advice.

In Denver I was examined from hair roots to toenails by a highly recommended physician, Dr. Randall Hodgson, whose mutton-chop whiskers were almost as impressive as his ample girth. This gentleman was thorough, considerate, and honest, well worth his substantial fee. I appreciated his candor but learned little.

After I dressed and joined him in his opulent office, Dr. Hodgson stared at the ceiling a moment, tented his fingers, and pronounced his verdict.

"Mister Saint Helen, in all honesty I do not have a definite diagnosis. There are many possibilities, but nothing I can test for or put my finger on at this time. I believe you have some early findings of a malady of the central nervous system. Exactly which malady I can not say. My advice to you would be to follow a good nutritious diet, limit your use of tobacco and alcohol, and let me see you again in six months. Unless, of course, the situation changes before then. In the meantime, you might benefit from hot mineral baths. I have heard anecdotal evidence they may be of benefit, although I have no definite scientific data. I am sorry, sir, I cannot be of more help, but"—he smiled genially—"often just the passage of time will give us the answers."

Perhaps I was not as forthright with the good doctor as I should have been, but I was reticent to speak of evanescent peculiarities I was experiencing for fear that he would think I was losing my mind.

Always I considered my personality to be rather volatile, to put it mildly, but I became aware of transient changes in my moods. Far less prone to anger and frustration, I was often gripped by an uplifting feeling of euphoria for no perceptible reason, so intense I regretted its passing.

During such raptures, I patted the babies of complete strangers, complimented unknown women on their lovely appearance, and gave excessive sums to beggars. From these heights I descended into the doldrums of disconsolation so unremitting that I confined myself to my room until they passed.

And with the depression, and sometimes with the euphoria, came the dreams or visions. I became a god-like figure directing the lives of all below me, or I saw Lincoln towering over me, shaking an accusatory bony finger in my face until his head exploded in a bloody mist. Sometimes I heard Robey calling from my grave: "Wrong, wrong!"

Then I was sane as a judge for weeks, months on end, with almost complete remittance of my physical symptoms. It was maddening.

But I did follow Dr. Hodgson's advice. Maybe a change of scenery was in order, for I had become restless again. Soon I would be immersed in the healing waters of Hot Springs, Arkansas.

Initially I considered a return visit to the baths at Glen Rose, but vanity dictated that I did not wish to see my old friends, or rather have them see me, in my present condition. Prior to leaving Denver, I began to follow Dr. Hodgson's prescriptions, minimizing alcohol consumption, eating regularly and well, and taking daily walks. The fleeting pain and clumsiness of my legs troubled me, but I persisted.

Travel by rail from Denver was a godsend. We rolled effortlessly across the verdant plains, covering in hours distances that had taken days only a few years ago. I arrived in Hot Springs reasonably refreshed. The disturbing dreams and visions had abated of their own volition, and my mood swings were less erratic.

For well over a month I followed a daily Spartan regimen consisting of horribly bland but nutritious foods, steeping my body for agonizing hours in the reeking sulphurous waters of Hades, and scrupulous avoidance of life's trinity of pleasure—tobacco, alcohol, and women. I feared the very flesh would be leached from my bones in the scalding baths, but was determined to stay the course. I did refuse with equal fortitude the prescription of daily enemas.

Weak as the proverbial kitten but remarkably free of my leg pains, I returned to Denver. *En route* I vowed honestly to apprise Dr. Hodgson of my troubling mental symptoms and again seek the advice of this physician who I trusted implicitly. I would, of course, not relate any incriminating details of my visions, hallucinations, or whatever these troubling thoughts might be.

"From this new information you have given me, Mister Saint Helen," Dr. Hodgson began after a forty-five minute interview and another head-to-toe physical examination, "I am now convinced your affliction of the central nervous system is diffuse, involving cognitive as well as motor function. Your reflexes and sensation in your lower extremities have definitely improved. I do feel your present regimen is beneficial, especially the hot baths. However, I am suspicious there has been a subtle, but detectable decline in cerebral function. Believe me, I am as anxious as you to have the answer, but at present I can only say that I have substantially narrowed the list of possible diagnoses. We can wait a little longer and see what develops, or, if money is no problem, I can refer you to the most astute neurologist on this planet, Doctor Jean Charcot in Paris."

In less than a month, telegraphic arrangements had been made with Dr. Charcot, I had journeyed by train to St. Louis, by paddlewheeler to New Orleans, boarded a fleet steamer to Cherbourg, and completed the trek by rail to Paris.

The supposed charm of this historic city completely escaped me. Some of its cathedrals are magnificent, it is true, but the overpowering body odor of its inhabitants completely obliterated any additional sensory input. A more liberal use of soap and water, instead of inadequate camouflage with offensive perfumes, would appreciably increase any non-resident's appreciation of the city's intellectual attractions.

Because of his international reputation, I presume, Professor Charcot employed a bevy of efficient translators who conveyed information to and from the doctor almost as fast as it was spoken. Dr. Hodgson's voluminous notes were read to him, then, Charcot queried me at length. For what seemed like hours, he painstakingly mapped my body with pinpricks, cotton wisps, glass vials of hot and cold water, and pounded me with tiny hammers. Each time I assumed he was finished, he would shine lights in my eyes, have me perform repetitive motions, and walk to and fro while he watched me intently, muttering to himself.

Next he attempted to mesmerize me as I gazed at a swinging locket but seemed very dissatisfied with his results, probably because of the distracting necessity of translating his murmured instructions.

I was then instructed to dress and was told Professor Charcot would see me the next day for a summation. But to complete today's examination, I was to be interrogated by one of his young associates, or students, I never knew which. This officious, bearded little Austrian immediately began bombarding me with brusque questions concerning my childhood and parentage so intimate my translator frequently stammered and blushed. When I heard he wished to know how long I had harbored repressed sexual desires toward my mother, I grasped his shirt front and tossed him bodily across the room. If I only had my Prescott with me, the career of this impertinent young Dr. Freud would have ended at that moment.

The following morning Professor Charcot seemed genuinely distressed at the grim news he relayed to me.

Syphilis. There is no known cause or cure. I may live for many years, or less than one year. My mind would probably deteriorate more rapidly than my body. He was very sorry and would send with me a full report to Dr. Hodgson, outlining his findings and the meager recommendations for my treatment.

I murmured my thanks and shuffled to the door like an automaton. At my accommodations, I stumbled through preparation for an immediate return to Denver and whatever the future might portend, crushed with the realization this would probably represent the last sea voyage of my life.

CHAPTER TWENTY-SIX

The long voyage home to Denver afforded me ample time to reflect on the prognosis given me by Dr. Charcot. Strangely I was not particularly distressed by the news, probably to a large degree because the uncertainty had ended. I knew my diagnosis and could make plans accordingly. The uncertain prognosis did not trouble me, for life itself is uncertain. I had always attempted to live each day to its fullest measure and would continue to do so. If and when the illness should limit this philosophy, I would unhesitatingly end my life without a moment of regret.

However, many tasks I had postponed or left undone were now insistent.

First and foremost, I should reëstablish some measure of rapport with my family, particularly Mother. Also, I must attempt to continue this journal, if necessary writing only on my lucid days. Dr. Hodgson should advise me concerning any future therapy. Money was no problem, I was very content with my accommodations, and would arrange for continued hydrotherapy in Denver if recommended by my doctor. Medical knowledge seemed to be advancing apace with the world-wide industrial revolution, so I could reasonably expect some breakthrough in the treatment of my condition might occur in the foreseeable future. I would not be disheartened. Although I was nearing fifty years of age, I did not feel old, and refused to curl up and die like a whipped dog.

Promptly after disembarking in New Orleans, I telegraphed Aunt Cordelia, asking her to arrange a propitious time and place for me to meet Mother, away from Joseph or any other family members, if possible. Mother would be nearly eighty years old, and travel for her might be difficult, so I emphasized that I would come to her at any site convenient and safe. My answer should be waiting by the time I reached Denver.

I had noticed on my voyage from Cherbourg that my gait was significantly more stable and the leg pains had almost completely disappeared. On the train to Denver I joined several card games to while away the time, and found my mental calculations had substantially improved. Dr. Charcot had advised me that my symptoms could conceivably wax and wane indefinitely, and apparently the good doctor was correct. Certainly my mental and physical condition on arrival in Denver was substantially improved over my circumstances at the time of my departure.

A note from Dr. Hodgson was waiting at my suite advising me to see him as soon as possible. No communication from Aunt Cordelia had yet arrived. I unpacked without delay and took a carriage to the doctor's office.

In spite of a waiting room glutted with patients, Dr. Hodgson's matronly nurse took my records and immediately ushered me into his examining room. I had barely settled in a comfortable chair when the doctor bustled in, his plump face glowing. Our usual friendly greetings were eschewed while he rapidly perused Dr. Charcot's report.

Suddenly he exulted: "I knew it, I knew it. The Great Masquerader. It was high on my list of diagnoses, but I refrained from mentioning it until my impression was confirmed. What did Charcot say about treatment?"

I repeated briefly what I had been told while the doctor nodded and leafed through the document.

"Yes, I certainly agree with Doctor Charcot. Mercury, our old stand-by, seems to cause more problems than it solves. You know, Mister Saint Helen, in these illnesses for which we have no satisfactory remedies, sooner or later almost everything reasonable"—he peered over his wire-rimmed glasses—"and unreasonable is tried. But in medicine our basic tenet is, first do no harm. So, that being the case, and in light of the fact that you seem to be improving or at least have entered a period of remission, I would agree with Doctor Charcot that we adhere to a plan of wait and see, watching you closely for any changes. Is that agreeable with you?"

I nodded my assent and, as instructed, made an appointment to see him three months hence. I would continue my walks, hot baths, and follow the righteous and sober life to which I had become grudgingly accustomed.

Then I began plans to visit Mother.

The telegram from Aunt Cordelia had initially been delivered to an incorrect address, but was waiting for me on my return.

Mary Ann passed away October 22 last year. Deepest sympathy. Cordelia.

Mother had been dead over a year and I did not know. I had not contacted her for fear of endangering her in some way. And now she was gone from my life forever.

I can write no more.

Months have passed since my last entry. Months spent wandering the wintry streets of Denver alone, experiencing true loneliness for the first time in my life. I refused to seek solace in bordellos or bottles as had been my practice in the past, for such acts would have been a travesty to Mother's memory. And, too, I must adhere to the doctors' mandates in hopes of avoiding exacerbations of my affliction.

During one of my idle meanderings I recalled with great sorrow my dear mother's unrealized lifelong ambition to become an actress. She was but a simple flower girl in London when father abandoned his wife and children and enticed Mother to flee with him to this country. I feel sure he, the unregenerate liar, would have promised her she would join him in starring rôles on the American stage. This promise was never kept.

After she bore him eleven children and tolerated his insane drunken rages for years, he married her only when he feared the scandal of their cohabitation might affect his career. Poor Mother was surrounded by a family of actors all her life and never fulfilled her own dreams of appearing on the stage with her renowned husband and sons.

I concluded the most appropriate memorial for dear Mother would be a provision whereby other frustrated actors and actresses could satisfy their yearnings.

With the assistance of a prestigious law firm recommended by Dr. Hodgson, I anonymously endowed a $100,000 scholarship fund for needy drama students.

Naturally I specified the endowment must be named for Mother, but realized the Booth name had been somewhat tainted. Therefore I utilized Mother's maiden name, and established the Mary Holmes Memorial Scholarship. I occasionally wonder if the many subsequent recipients of this largess would be as grateful if they were aware of its provider. Probably it would make no difference, for actors are a peculiar bunch.

This bit of philanthropy piqued a resurgence of my interest in the theatre. Initially I volunteered for work in local productions with the backstage crews, but, as my talents became obvious, I found myself serving as mentor to the novices, then directing and actually performing in minor rôles. Now that I was in my fifties, I particularly relished the comfortable portrayals of more mature characters, rather than the fiery personations for which I was so famous in my youth. Offstage I gently rebuffed the inevitable flirtations from the youthful ingénues, but enjoyed a succession of festive transient relationships with actresses nearer my own age, vastly more experienced and inevitably more appreciative.

Dr. Hodgson found no evidence of deterioration or new findings on my biannual evaluations, and I had experienced no progression of the mental symptoms which had so concerned me in months past. However, I was aware of an almost constant suffusion of mild euphoria, a welcome replacement for the dark moods that haunted my earlier years. But my restless spirit remained as potent as ever. Periodically I would take leave of the theatre and travel to a distant land, just for the sheer rapture of change, new faces, and new experiences. If the spirit so moved me, I would be accompanied by a paramour of the moment, but most often I traveled alone.

The Taj Mahal illuminated by a full moon, the Pyramids, the Amazon to its headwaters, I viewed them all. Each time I would return to Denver thinking I would quietly and gracefully grow old, wanderlust would rear its irresistible head, and I would be gone again. My lavish tastes in food, wardrobe, and accommodations were the stuff of legend. I denied myself nothing that money could buy, and I was blessed with a plenitude of funds. Such flamboyant behavior ensured that I never lacked companionship.

The years have flown by, but my least concern was the passage of time. I made each day unique and one to remember.

The dawn of our 20th Century I welcomed by hosting a sumptuous banquet for a motley collection of recent acquaintances and total strangers in Anchorage, Alaska. Why I visited there in the first place is still a mystery, but I had a wonderful time. When I returned to Denver, my plan was to rest and remain idle for a spell, but fate deemed otherwise.

Buffalo Bill's Wild West Show had returned from a triumphant tour of England and once again was performing in Denver. I had encountered many advertisements of this production in the past but had had no desire to attend a spectacle of simulated battles, trick riders, and pungent livestock. But friends at the theatre insisted I accompany them if for nothing more than to solicit my opinion on the feasibility of adapting such a monumentally successful and panoramic drama to the indoor stage.

I had expected to meet a pompous charlatan, but Buffalo Bill, a.k.a. William Cody, was as charming as he was physically impressive. Much taller than I, dressed in immaculate buckskins, his flowing moustache and goatee matching snow-white hair cascading stylishly to his broad shoulders, he was the epitome of a consummate showman.

But I was considerably more impressed with his courtly manners and concern with the welfare of his troupe, particularly the livestock. And, much against public sentiment at the time, he showered the Indians in his employ with genuine affection and admiration. Despite blistering editorials in newspapers maligning him, he continued to reiterate his revisionist views concerning Custer's last stand. In his opinion, and mine, this episode was not a slaughter of courageous outnumbered Federal troops by bloodthirsty savages, but a successful defense by skilled warriors against yet another incursion upon their homeland.

Bill and I became friends immediately, each recognizing something of one's self in the other.

I was able to contribute insightful and valuable suggestions to enhance the drama of his production; in return, I was given a reserved seat in Bill's private box for each performance, occasionally played minor rôles, and was fêted by his cast.

With the possible exception of Cody himself, my favorite trouper, of course, was "Little Sure Shot", Annie Oakley. Offstage a rather shy lady devoted to her husband, her legendary skills with firearms were truly amazing. Although she was entering her forties when I first made her acquaintance, her talents showed no signs of diminishing. I am sure age, lack of practice, and possibly my malady had taken their toll, for the best I could manage in occasional impromptu matches with Annie was a tie.

Fate again smiled upon me. After watching our friendly competition, Bill begged me to join the show, but I had no desire to waste ammunition on blocks of wood and glass balls. Less than a year later, Annie and many others of her troupe were involved in a tragic train accident. She received severe spinal injuries, but I was able substantially to assist in arranging preëminent surgical care for her and she recovered fully after several operations. Her shooting expertise never faltered. Among my most treasured possessions are the simply worded but eloquent thank you notes from this dear lady.

CHAPTER TWENTY-SEVEN

Since early childhood I have always been an avid reader, priding myself on speed and comprehension. As a young man I devoured the works of Shakespeare and other classics, generally avoiding the turgid prose of popular literature. Of course, during my professional career, I buried myself almost exclusively in dramas. In later years I discovered the magic of novels and poems, particularly those of my friends Oscar Wilde and Sam Clemens.

In general I avoided newspapers as much as possible and scanned them only to be reasonably conversant with current events. Even the best of their efforts tended to contain poorly written and often inaccurate accounts of life's unpleasant aspects. Wars, murders, and shenanigans filled their pages to nurture, I suppose, the limited intellect of their editors and faithful readers. Poor Oscar's scandalous trial and imprisonment, the war with Spain, corruption in Washington, double-dealing by railroad barons—the litany of reported transgressions was endless.

Some years before, obscured by news of Theodore Roosevelt and the battles in Cuba, I happened upon a short series of laughably inaccurate articles claiming John Wilkes Booth was alive and allegedly living in South America. Except as a transient source of amusement, I had dismissed such drivel from my memory.

But now, in 1902, I read a piece in the Denver *Post* concerning an itinerant carpenter named David George from Oklahoma, of all places, who claimed to be John Wilkes

Booth. To my astonishment, this blather greatly disturbed me. It was readily apparent the article's author, whose name was not given, did not believe George's assertion and implied the man was obviously demented. Certainly this would seem reasonable, for who in their right mind would claim to be me and suffer the certain vilification and probable physical abuse that would follow. With George's unsullied background, he could have more logically claimed to be Jesus, rather than Satan incarnate.

According to the article, two years earlier this George person had attempted suicide by ingesting a large quantity of medication while living in El Reno, Oklahoma. On his supposed deathbed he confessed to a Miss Young he was "the man who killed Lincoln." When George recovered, he promptly fled El Reno and now allegedly lived in nearby Enid.

I would teach this imposter a lesson. If he assumed this rôle in hopes of some personal gain through notoriety, I could demonstrate the dangers of such a pose. If he were truly demented, my appearance might convince him his fantasy was just that, the delusion of a disturbed mind.

A brief visit to the theatre allowed me to select a stylish outfit appropriate for the 1860s and my elaborate make-up kit. These were packed with my usual wardrobe and, just in case, I carried my Prescott in its shoulder holster.

Upon arrival in Enid the week after New Year's Day, 1903, I obtained barely adequate lodgings in the town's best hotel and began to make discreet inquiries about this David George.

He and I were roughly the same age and size; he was far from illiterate as I had imagined, and, to my astonishment, while in El Reno he had appeared several times in productions of the local theatre. Apparently the man had access to an occult source of income, for he dressed fashionably, puffed imported cheroots, and imbibed only the finest whiskey. He had also suffered a broken leg and frequently carried a cane, but my informant was unsure which leg George had fractured.

In little more than a week, I had completed my research and finalized my plan. Mr. George was given an appointment to visit me in my hotel room with the prospect of being selected for an upcoming stage production in Enid. I began my transformation.

With the artful application of make-up, I subtracted over thirty years from my countenance, aided by dying my hair a raven's black, and applying a drooping dark moustache. I donned raiment borrowed from the theatre and compared my mirror image with an old tintype of me taken in my late twenties. The resemblance was perfect.

When I opened the door for David George, I am unsure which of us was more stunned, but I was far the better actor and concealed my astonishment. I saw in him the mirror image of myself as I truly was while he saw the image of his fantasies.

"Please come in, Mister George," I said with a gracious bow. "I am John Wilkes Booth."

The stricken man dropped like a stone into the chair, and, for a moment, I feared his heart had stopped. In that instant his delusion was shattered forever. Reality cruelly bludgeoned his assumed persona into nothingness. Now he was forced to admit to himself that his past fantasy of being me was solely the product of his diseased mind.

For a split second his pathetic visage evoked a twinge of sympathy, but then I pressed on. After all, I was John Wilkes Booth; he was but a crazy man who thought he was.

"I shall return," I said in my most sepulchral tones, "in your waking hours and your tortured dreams. You will never be rid of me. You have taken my body for your own, but I have taken your immortal soul."

I shrieked a maniacal laugh while the demented fool fled from my room.

On the night of January 13th, 1903, David George, alone in his room, drank poison, convulsed, and died.

Fate had deemed yet another macabre twist in this small prairie town. The infamous Boston Corbett, my supposed executioner, had been in and out of mental institutions since his ephemeral notoriety in the late 1860s. After all, this was a man so mentally disturbed he had castrated himself with a pair of scissors at age nineteen to avoid temptation from prostitutes. Obsessed with matters religious, in recent years he had become a ranting street evangelist spouting his deranged message to meager audiences mildly amused by his strange behavior. Now he was in Enid. He also deserved a visit from the young Wilkes Booth.

I reprised my make-up and costume and joined the few onlookers so starved for entertainment they tolerated his ungrammatical and erroneous interpretations of the Scriptures. When he finished his mercifully brief oration and his bored listeners had moved on, I stepped close to him and smiled.

"Hello, Mister Corbett, I am John Wilkes Booth. You killed the wrong man."

His eyes almost leaped from their sockets. He jabbered insanely, spittle dripping from his lips, then fled down the rutted street, flailing his arms wildly and shrieking gibberish. Later that same day I learned he had been arrested for his erratic behavior and proceedings were in motion for his immediate re-admission to an insane asylum.

Soon after my return to Denver, events in tiny Enid, Oklahoma were front page news. The body of David George had been transferred to the Penniman Funeral Home and was identified as John Wilkes Booth by a Reverend Harper who was conducting a funeral there. Harper based this identification on the fact that this David George had confessed in El Reno to his wife, the former Miss Young, that he was Booth.

Apparently the body lay unclaimed. Less than two weeks later the papers announced the arrival of Finis Bates, a lawyer from Memphis, who identified George's body as a friend of his, John St. Helen, who had confessed to him that he was really John Wilkes Booth. For the first time I learned that this supposed friend I had trusted so implicitly years ago in Texas had attempted to collect a reward by turning me in to the authorities following my sickbed confession to him. But agents of the government had not believed Bates's tale and refused his offer.

Now this slimy necrophiliac was once again attempting to profit from the legacy of John Wilkes Booth, this time by defiling the dead. He financed the mummification of David George's body, purchased the mummy, and arranged for it to be shipped back to Memphis. I am sure he planned some manner of profitable, albeit repulsive exhibition of George's remains, claiming the mummy to be Lincoln's assassin.

CHAPTER TWENTY-EIGHT

On the train returning to Denver from the sojourn to Enid, my sight began to fail. The changes initially were so subtle I was unable to determine the precise time of their onset, but, on walking to the carriage after my arrival, I also noted some unsteadiness of gait. Whether this was due to the impairment of vision or further neurological deterioration, I could not determine.

One would think such symptoms would have alarmed me, but my usual euphoria had become even more intense. With a strangely detached view, I regarded these new developments as inconsequential and mildly amusing. However, when I visited Dr. Hodgson nearly a month later for my routine appointment, he was not amused.

Once again I was bombarded with his silly questions regarding my recollection of time, place, random words, and numbers. I was asked to identify common objects by name, spell words backwards, and interpret several proverbs. I considered my numerous errors to be hilarious. Frequently I caught myself offering vague and implausible excuses for my poor performance.

Next I was subjected to the doctor's relentless assault on my person with annoying pinpricks, cotton wisps, and tuning forks, followed by percussion of my peripheral joints with foolish little hammers.

Dr. Hodgson allowed me to dress, and I joined him in his comfortable office. As was his custom when an oration was pending, he stared at the ceiling for a time, his fingers tented under his chin, then leaned forward to face me. He looked suddenly very old beyond his years.

"Mister Saint Helen, the remission is over. Since your last visit, six months ago significant physical, and I am sad to say, mental deterioration has occurred. I am afraid we have reached the slippery slope of rapidly declining function I have so long feared."

He lowered his head for a moment and massaged the nape of his neck with his hand, then his sad eyes looked deep into mine.

"I have no treatment . . . I have no cure. But I can assure you I shall do everything medically possible to guarantee your comfort"—he paused and cleared his throat—"from now until. . . ."

I burst out laughing.

My reaction to Hodgson's grim prognosis rocked the good doctor back in his chair. An incredulous expression spread over his countenance.

When I was able to suppress my chuckling, I managed a response. "I am sorry, Doctor Hodgson, but you looked so serious. And never before have I been offered any sort of a guarantee by a physician. Besides, for a man who can neither walk nor see well, I feel fine."

Dr. Hodgson did not return my smirk and again leaned forward in his chair. He spoke as if he were lecturing an inept student.

"Mister Saint Helen, I have no desire to burst your bubble needlessly, but I must convince you that your inappropriate sense of well-being and lack of concern are particularly disturbing manifestations of far advanced disease of the brain. Doctor Charcot refers to this as *'la belle indifferance'*. Although some might regard this manifestation as a blessing, its appearance concerns me deeply. Certainly

I do not wish to paint too bleak a picture, but I know you as a man possessing considerable assets and no strong family ties. Therefore, please do not consider me too presumptuous when I strongly advise you to put your affairs in order before further . . . ah . . . mental problems arise which might affect your judgment. Do you follow me?"

Although I still felt somewhat giddy as if I had ingested too much brandy, I regained my composure.

"As always, Doctor, I appreciate your candor and advice, which I shall follow at the earliest instant. But be not dismayed, my dear Doctor, I have conquered dragons far more formidable. Shall I visit you again one month hence?"

He nodded slowly while chewing meditatively on his lower lip as if he wished to speak again, but appropriate words seemed to have evaded him.

Before sundown that day, I had visited my banker and assayed my financial status. Despite my rather extravagant life style over the past few years, my net worth had appreciably increased.

Next, I visited my skilled, obsequious attorneys and instructed them to double my endowment in the Mary Holmes Trust. I would arrange for the distribution of the remaining balance of my considerable assets after further reflection.

Well aware of Finis Bates's despicable plans to exploit the body of the supposed John Wilkes Booth, I could easily imagine the desecration of my remains should they somehow be identified. The attorneys prepared an iron-clad document to the effect that my body would be cremated immediately after death, the ashes pulverized and cast to the winds off Prospect Point in the nearby Rocky Mountains.

I made it abundantly clear that I did not wish this action

to be delayed by any type of religious services. I had shattered each of the Ten Commandments, some of them repeatedly, and was not so hypocritical as to expect any absolution on this earth, or mercy should there be an afterlife.

Upon completion of these mundane but necessary tasks, I proposed to devote my waking hours solely to the pursuit of pleasure. Although I must admit that none of life's exquisite joys had escaped my enthusiastic participation in years past, several warranted further sampling.

But even the euphoria could not completely blind me to the precipitous increase in my physical limitations, especially walking any appreciable distance or managing a horse and carriage.

It has been said that angels often arrive when they are least expected and most needed. Mine certainly did, but most assuredly not in the form I would have anticipated.

Monumental in size and bearing with a skin far from alabaster, the laundress I have employed for a number of years noted one morning my struggles to seat myself into the buggy. She rushed to my assistance. When I returned much later from the lawyers' office, she had waited to help me to my room, return the rig to the livery stable, and bring my evening meal on a tray from the dining room. Such pampering is a welcome relief from my stubborn struggles to remain completely independent, and, before the evening ended, this widowed giantess had convinced me I needed her ministrations on a daily basis. She refused to speak of remuneration, saying simply: "I just like to hep folks that needs me."

From that day on she was available for my every want. I suspected she must possess the gift of prophesy, for my condition had rapidly plummeted into an inexorable downward spiral. I was unable to walk unassisted, my speech was garbled, and my thoughts erratic. But I insisted on being driven into the mountains through the early flurries of snow to Prospect Point for a final glimpse of my beloved mountains.

My black angel understood, and we made the journey seated together wrapped in blankets, studiously ignoring the shocked expressions and turned heads of those we passed. This brief trip afforded me an opportunity to make definite decisions on issues I had been mentally debating for some time. Now I had to act fast.

The time had come for my final visit with Dr. Hodgson. This great and good man had become much more than a physician to me. I regarded him as a true friend and thus spoke to him with complete candor.

I had decided to end my own life. All too often I had seen the ghastly effects of gunshot wounds and did not wish to subject my angel to the discovery of such a horrific scene. I asked Dr. Hodgson, therefore, to provide me with the means to exit this world without pain, without prolongation, and without unpleasantness.

I was sure I detected a glint of tears in his eyes as the doctor replied. "Mister Saint Helen, John, I cannot do what you ask. As much as I agree with your decision, despite my religious beliefs, and as much as I would like to help you, I must not. To do so would violate the principles and ethics on which I have based the practice of medicine throughout my entire career. I am sorry, my friend."

Once again he gazed at the ceiling, hands prayerfully folded under his chin, then stared into my eyes as if he could read my thoughts.

"However, it is an extremely important facet of your

treatment that you rest well at night. Therefore, I am prescribing a rather large flask of tincture of opium . . . laudanum. You should take several drams of this every evening to insure a good night's sleep. Only a few drams, mind you."

He reached across the desk and clasped both my hands in his.

"For should you drink the entire flask, you would go quietly and peacefully to sleep, but would never awaken. Do you understand me?"

I nodded, unable to speak.

CHAPTER TWENTY-NINE

The lawyers have divided my considerable assets between a permanently endowed scholarship fund in Dr. Hodgson's name for needy medical students and a lifelong annuity for my angel. She asked for nothing; now she will never want for anything. Even in my journal she will remain nameless. I wish for her to enjoy this legacy in peace.

I now write my final entry. The flask is empty. I sit, pen in hand, but find no appropriate words to leave, no wisdom to share.

I have killed in self-defense; I have killed for hire; I have killed in anger. But I never killed a man who did not deserve to die . . . save one.

I never intended to kill Abraham Lincoln.

EPILOGUE

"So, what do you think? Is Booth's journal authentic?"

Ken turned from his keyboard and frowned for a moment.

"Yes, now I am convinced he wrote it, so the story of his surviving the barn episode obviously is based on facts. But I'm still not persuaded his account is entirely truthful. He was an extremely histrionic character, to say the least."

"No doubt about that. But how did Booth's journal end up in his imposter's mummy?"

Ken turned back to his word processor. "Pres, as I said early on, there's a lot no one will ever know about John Wilkes Booth."

ACKNOWLEDGMENTS

Sincere thanks to my mentors and friends, Ken Casper and Ken Hodgson, for their encouragement and guidance. I could not have done it without them.

Special thanks to Suzanne Campbell and staff at the West Texas Collection for their invaluable assistance with research.

ABOUT THE AUTHOR

Preston Darby was born and raised in Columbia, South Carolina. He graduated from the University of South Carolina in 1950 and the Medical College of South Carolina in 1954. After nearly ten years in the Air Force as a flight surgeon and then as an internist, he entered civilian practice in Big Spring, Texas, and moved to San Angelo in 1969. Dr. Darby is the author of numerous scientific articles, newspaper essays, and short stories. In 1994, he published the book, *Tears of the Oppressed: An American Doctor in Afghanistan*, detailing his experiences as a physician in Afghanistan during the Soviet invasion. *The Reluctant Assassin* is his first published work of fiction. Now retired, he lives in San Angelo.